D1206238

OH! TO BE IN ENGLAND

ALSO BY H. E. BATES

Novels

THE TWO SISTERS
CHARLOTTE'S ROW
THE POACHER
SPELLA HO
THE CRUISE OF THE
  BREADWINNER
THE JACARANDA TREE
LOVE FOR LYDIA
THE SLEEPLESS MOON
THE DARLING BUDS OF MAY
A BREATH OF FRENCH AIR
WHEN THE GREEN WOODS LAUGH
THE DAY OF THE TORTOISE

CATHERINE FOSTER
THE FALLOW LAND
A HOUSE OF WOMEN
FAIR STOOD THE WIND
  FOR FRANCE
THE PURPLE PLAIN
THE SCARLET SWORD
THE NATURE OF LOVE
THE FEAST OF JULY
DEATH OF A HUNTSMAN
AN ASPIDISTRA IN
  BABYLON
THE GOLDEN ORIOLE

A CROWN OF WILD MYRTLE

Short Stories

DAY'S END
THE BLACK BOXER
CUT AND COME AGAIN
THE FLYING GOAT
THE BRIDE COMES TO
  EVENSFORD
COLONEL JULIAN
THE WATERCRESS GIRL

SEVEN TALES AND ALEXANDER
THE WOMAN WHO HAD
  IMAGINATION
SOMETHING SHORT AND SWEET
THE BEAUTY OF THE DEAD
DEAR LIFE
THE DAFFODIL SKY
NOW SLEEPS THE CRIMSON PETAL

Drama
THE DAY OF GLORY

Essays

FLOWERS AND FACES
DOWN THE RIVER
THE HEART OF THE COUNTRY
THE COUNTRY HEART

THROUGH THE WOODS
THE SEASONS AND THE GARDENER
O! MORE THAN HAPPY COUNTRYMAN
THE COUNTRY OF WHITE CLOVER

EDWARD GARNETT: A MEMOIR

Collections of Short Stories
THIRTY TALES
MY UNCLE SILAS
(Illustrated by Edward Ardizzone)
COUNTRY TALES
SUGAR FOR THE HORSE
(Illustrated by Edward Ardizzone)

Criticism
THE MODERN SHORT STORY

As 'Flying Officer X'
THE GREATEST PEOPLE IN THE WORLD
HOW SLEEP THE BRAVE

H. E. Bates

Oh!
To Be in England

NEW YORK | FARRAR, STRAUS AND COMPANY

Copyright © 1963 by Evensford Productions Ltd.
Library of Congress catalog card number 64-11452
First Printing, 1964
Manufactured in the U.S.A.

823.91
B329o

This book
is
dedicated
to
STEPHEN

JEREMY

ANDREW

BEVERLEY

and

EMMA

1

As Pop Larkin loaded the last pieces of junk into his newly painted yellow-and-scarlet pick-up all the essence of the fine June morning seemed to pour down like dreamy honey from thick boughs of oak-flower, gold-green against a sky of purest blue, unblemished except for a few floating white doves of cloud. It was a morning when he felt it was good to be alive; you could fairly hear the grass growing. All the air was brilliant with bird song and farther up the road, on a little rise, a field thick with buttercups shone brighter than a bank of sovereigns.

'Well, I think that's the lot, Lady Violet. Quite sure you're satisfied?'

'Oh! absolutely, Mr Larkin. Absolutely—'

'Because now's the time to say if you ain't. I want to be fair.'

'Oh! you've been more than fair, Mr Larkin. More than fair, I assure you. The offer I had from two men from London was far, far less.'

'Never trust blokes from London,' Pop said, quite sternly. 'Never trust Londoners. Not at no price.'

Lady Violet stood with a kind of hungry frailty in the sunshine, rather like a small brownish moth wearing gold-rimmed spectacles. Soft wisps of sepia whiskers grew about her face, giving it a curious downy charm.

Pop took a cigar from his breast pocket and started to pierce the end of it with the gold-plated cutter Ma had given him for Christmas. Sometimes he used it to pick his teeth with too, but Ma really didn't like the habit very much. It was a bit primitive, she thought.

'Well, I'll just run over the lot again,' Pop said, 'just to see I've got everything. One bassinet—'

'Oh! I was wheeled about in that bassinet. So was my sister. I tipped her out of it on many occasions.'

'One butter churn—'

'I used to help turn the handle in the dairy. Every Wednesday and Saturday. I can hear the flop-flop now.'

'One hip-bath. One foot-bath—'

'I think they're sweet, don't you? Especially the foot-bath, with the pink roses. They're Regency, you know. I suppose nobody ever uses them today?'

'Put flowers into 'em,' Pop said. The Regency wash-basin, the two Regency ewers and the three Regency chamber pots all had pink roses on them too. 'Two bedsteads and a knife cleaner. One secretaire and two oak chests. Two stags' heads and one pike in glass case. Two shields and four battle-axes—'

'And of course the two suits of armour. I must say I think it was wonderfully noble of you to take the suits of armour. I never thought you would.'

Pop, blandly waving the still unlit cigar, warmly assured her that he was very glad to have the suits of armour. They were the prize pieces of the lot: just what he'd been looking for.

'You don't think you'll have difficulty in finding a customer for them?'

'Customer?' Pop said. 'Customer? I got one already. Me.'

The two suits of armour were going to stand in the passage at home, one each side of the sitting-room door. Pop had the picture of them already quite clear in his mind. The two shields and the four battle-axes were to hang each side of them. He might even fit the vizors up with lights, he thought, or if they were too big for the passage they could stand outside the front door, on sentry, sort of. Wherever they stood they'd certainly give some tone.

'Well, I think that's the lot. Oh! the buggy, of course. I'll have to make a special trip to fetch the buggy. I'll have to have my son Montgomery come and give me a hand with that.'

'The dear buggy. I've ridden in it so often.'

'Tell you what. Me and Ma'll come and fetch you out for a ride in it one Sunday. Now if you're perfickly satisfied I'll settle up with you.'

Pop stuck the unlit cigar into his mouth and then produced from his inside pocket a roll of five-pound notes as thick as a fair-sized bible.

'Oh! you must come in and have a glass of sherry before you go. Or port. I've got one or the other. I'm not sure which. Do, please.'

Lady Violet turned and led the way into the cramped spaces of a wooden bungalow surrounded by unkempt beds of purple lupins, pink and white paeonies and a few early roses. It didn't seem to Pop much larger than a decent dog kennel and as he went inside he found himself suddenly overcome by an irremediable sadness.

It was the same feeling he got sometimes when he was talking to his old friend the Brigadier. It hurt him to see the top people coming down so low. He could remember without difficulty the time when Lady Violet and her family had lived in a big black-and-white half-timbered house with a moat round it and great splendid stables and farm-barns as dignified as old cathedrals. He supposed change was inevitable but there were times when he didn't hold with it being so drastic, especially here in England.

'I won't be a minute with the sherry. And do you prefer a cheesy biscuit or a ginger nut?'

Pop confessed he preferred the ginger nut; he was a sweet-toothed man.

While waiting for the sherry to arrive he stared about him. There was a great shabbiness in the air. The dust that lay everywhere on furniture, mantelpiece and carpet was, like Lady Violet's soft brown whiskers, thick as down on moth wings. Horse hair sprouted from the arms and seats of chairs. A dish of primroses, now brown dried emblems of an already distant April, stood on a window sill, forgotten. A few rings of apple-peel, yellow and shrivelled, lay scattered about the hearth, above which a large barn owl in a mahogany case stared out with big saucer eyes, for ever spiritlessly searching. Pop felt sure the floor was rotting underneath him. The air was full of a church-like odour of decay and he longed to light his cigar.

'It was sherry after all. And there are the ginger nuts.' Lady Violet handed Pop the smallest possible thimble of sweet sherry and he helped himself to a ginger nut. 'Good health to you.'

Pop thanked her and said 'Cheers, Lady Violet, and down the hatch,' and could have sworn at the same time that there was dust on the ginger nut too. He felt he wouldn't get very steamed up on the sherry either and for a few painful moments he longed not only for the luxury of his cigar but for a pint of Dragon's Blood or a decent cocktail. During the past week he'd invented a pretty good new one consisting of two parts vodka to three of rye whisky with a dash of rum and Kirsch to warm up the flavour. He'd christened it Moon-Rocket and he thought on the whole it went down pretty well.

'Mind if I light my cigar? Wouldn't offend you?'

'Oh! dear, no. Of course not. Please do. I adore the smell of cigars.'

Suddenly full of mischievous entreaty, Pop gave a scarcely perceptible wink, his eye-lid swift as a dragonfly, and made the suggestion that perhaps Lady Violet might even care for one herself? Did she indulge? – he meant on the quiet like?

Lady Violet gave the merest echo of a giggle and her small eyes dithered in tremulous response behind her glasses.

'Well, I don't really. But I do confess that I once took several teeny-weeny puffs of one of my father's.'

'Like it?'

'I'm ashamed to say that I did. Rather much.'

Pop gave his first good real laugh of the day and started to light his cigar, feeling better already. He didn't often get the willies about junk – it was just impersonal stuff, most times – but the sight of a leaking wood-shed half-filled with the suits of armour, the old buggy, the butter churn and even the chamber pots had got him under the skin somehow. It was like seeing another bit of England go.

He puffed richly, filling the little room with smoke, and then, full of mischief, winked again, this time broadly.

'Have a draw, Lady Violet. Go on.'

Lady Violet, at the mere suggestion of having a draw, flushed quite deeply. It was as if she had been caught out in some awful act of impropriety.

'Mr Larkin, you're quite outrageous—'

'Course I am. What of it? You said you liked 'em. Go on, have a draw. A little bit of what you fancy—'

'I was only sixteen when I did it before.'

'Don't look much older now.' Lady Violet, who was on the verge of becoming seventy-five, felt flattered into a sudden spasm of mischief of her own and made an impetuous grab at the cigar.

'All right. You dared me to. I always loved a dare.'

'Have a good old drag,' Pop said. 'Do you all the good in the world.'

Lady Violet, powerfully tempted for one moment to take Pop at his word, finally decided on prudence and merely puffed discreetly.

'Quite delicious.'

'Glad you like it. I thought you would. Best Havana.'

'Thank you very much. You'd better have it back now. You've tempted me quite enough.'

Pop, laughing again with all his customary ringing heartiness, said he liked tempting girls, at the same time resisting a strong temptation to pat her playfully.

'No, keep it. Have another go while I count the money out. What did I say for the lot? – sixty-five quid? Call it seventy. The jerries alone are worth another fiver. Ma'll be tickled to death with 'em – ring-a-ring-a-roses, eh?'

Lady Violet, still puffing gently, smiled down at the thick wedge of notes from which Pop was counting out her money.

'I heard someone say the other day that they're actually coming back into fashion again.'

'Never been out as far as Ma's concerned! Well, there you are then, seventy quid. Better count it to see if it's right.'

'I don't think I need to, Mr Larkin. I trust you implicitly.'

'Just as well somebody does. Well, I must be on the trot. Thank you for everything. Like to keep the cigar?'

'Oh! certainly not. I wouldn't dream of such a thing.'

'Course you would. Keep it. Plenty more at home.'

'I must say it's absolutely delicious. It's absolutely made my day.'

'Perfick,' Pop said. 'Perfick. That's what I like to hear.'

Lady Violet tottered gently as far as the front door of the bungalow to say good-bye to him, the cigar still alight in her hand. The frailty of the downy face, with its air of groping hunger, seemed for fully half a minute to disappear. The small eyes were now quite brilliant behind the gold rims of her spectacles. Framed against the gimcrack door she looked positively alight with life and there was something almost jaunty about the way she waved the cigar.

'Good-bye!' Pop said. 'Thanks again. Be over for the buggy tomorrow.'

'Good-bye, Mr Larkin – Oh! no, not tomorrow. I've just remembered. I have to entertain my niece and nephew tomorrow. They're coming to stay for Whitsun.'

'Not to worry,' Pop said. 'Make it the day after.'

'Splendid. Thank you again for all you've done. Good-bye.'

Cigarless but happy himself, Pop drove slowly home through narrow lanes thick with green-white kex, each head like stiff fragile lace, and by woods of bluebells heavy with the deep eternal perfume that never failed to set all his senses quivering.

It had been a very good morning. It was good to be alive, better still to be alive in England. He chuckled to himself several times about the armour and also wondered what Ma would say to the ring-a-ring-a-roses.

He couldn't help thinking they'd look very nice with hyacinths in them for Christmas.

2

After quenching his thirst with a steady quart of shandy at *The Hare & Hounds* Pop arrived home in the expectation of finding Ma in the kitchen, surrounded as always by dishes, saucepans and piles of food. His eager mating call of 'Hullo, hullo, where's my old sunflower?' remained, however, unanswered; and it was some minutes before he discovered her in the garden, where she had set up easel, canvas, paint box and camp stool and was busy painting a picture of Mariette in the nude. She seemed fatter and rounder than ever, sitting on the tiny camp stool.

When she saw Pop crossing the garden Mariette deftly but with otherwise no great concern, covered her resplendent and now maternal nakedness with *The Daily Mirror*, which in turn linked up with the only garment she was wearing, a pair of transparent purple briefs with lace edges. Having given birth two months before to a boy who, at Ma's suggestion, had been named John Marlborough Churchill Blenheim Charlton, she was now anxious to coax her figure back to its normal splendid proportions and to get it, if possible, brown all over. The result was that Ma was now doing a different picture of her almost every other day, either from the front, the back or the sides, according to which part of her was most in the need of being sun-tanned. Mr Charlton found the canvases of intense and palpitating interest, so much so that he had had two of them, one a full-blooded frontal view, the other a horizontal back view of Mariette lying among buttercups, framed.

'Hullo, hullo,' Pop said. 'Art class? Very nice too. How's it coming on?'

Looking over Ma's shoulder he surveyed, with something more than paternal pride, the stunning contours of Mariette's upper figure as seen by Ma. It was six months since Ma had taken up painting, largely because practically everyone else, from Churchill downwards, had taken it up too. She was surprisingly good at it, everyone thought. She had also read the great man's little book on the subject and as well as being inspired to name the new baby after him had also taken his advice to revel in paint as a physical luxury.

'Bit blue, ain't they, Ma?'

Greatly though he admired Ma's newly revealed talents, there were times when he thought she might be going a bit too modern. The splendour of Mariette's upper contours looked, he thought, not only as blue as cornflowers but also a bit lop-sided somehow, but he supposed it all depended on how you looked at them. The artist's eye and all that.

'Well, they're no bluer than you'll be if you don't soon make yourself scarce so's I can get another look at them. Go and get yourself a drink, do. I can't very well see through *The Daily Mirror*, can I?'

Pop cordially agreed, at the same time blandly suggesting that he himself had no objection if Mariette wanted to take *The Daily Mirror* away. What did it matter? It was all one to him. It was all in the family.

'By the way,' Mariette said, 'there's some letters for you. One of them with a foreign stamp on.'

'That's it,' Ma said, 'go and read your letters. And bring us both a decent cold drink when you come back. It's hot out here in the sun.'

Making a final survey of Mariette's shining blue breasts Pop suddenly announced that he had a good mind to take up the painting lark himself. He knew Mr Charlton was thinking of taking it up too.

'You should,' Ma said. 'It's a wonderful thing. It's so soothing. There's nothing like it for passing the time.'

A second later an electrifying thought occurred to Pop: none other than that if he took up painting it might be possible to get somebody like Angela Snow to sit for him as a model. In the never-never, of course. Did Ma think she would?

Ma, with complete unconcern, said she didn't see why not. Pop should ask her.

'Daresay she'd love to be painted by you. By the way, how did you get on with Lady Violet? She's no oil painting, poor thing.'

'Perfick,' Pop said. 'Got two suits of armour and two sets of shields and battle-axes. Thought they'd look nice in the passage. Oh! and a present for you.'

'That's nice,' Ma said, as if suits of armour, shields and battle-axes were no more unusual than apples, oranges and pears. 'Give me a kiss.'

Pop promptly kissed Ma full on the lips, not with his usual protracted and burning intensity but rather as if casually taking a little light refreshment.

'Still think they're a bit too blue, Ma.'

'Well, they're going to be pinked up a bit in a minute if you'll make yourself scarce so I can get on with it. Go and get the drinks, do.'

While Pop had gone into the house to fetch both drinks and letters Ma proceeded to touch in a few pink lights on the upper edges of Mariette's breasts, remarking at the same time:

'Suits of armour, eh? Going baronial and all that. Next thing you know we'll be having a butler.'

Five minutes later Pop came back from the house carrying a tray of drinks and his letters in one hand and one of the three Regency chamber-pots in the other. Ma started shaking and laughing like a ripe jelly and Mariette in turn was so overcome with cascades of laughter that for a moment she forgot all about *The Daily Mirror*, with the result that Pop had a brief and satisfying glimpse of his eldest daughter as Nature had made her. It merely served to convince him that Ma was altogether wrong about the blue, though he didn't like to say so.

Ma now surveyed the rose-ringed chamber-pot with tearful eyes.

'What am I supposed to do with that?' she said.

Pop remarked blandly that he thought hyacinths would look nice in it for Christmas, or tulips or something. There were three of them. They were very old. Regency.

'Well, they'll come in handy for something, that's

certain,' Ma said and broke once again into rich, ripe laughter.

'They're all the fashion now,' Pop said, 'these Regency things.'

'Now you've gone and put me off,' Ma said and proceeded to lay her brushes and palette down on her paint box, afterwards wiping her hands on a piece of rag. 'I'll carry on after lunch. You'd better run and put your dress on, dear. And see if little Oscar's awake and if he is bring him down.'

Pop had made a jugful of his new Moon-Rocket, double strength as usual, with plenty of ice, and he now gave it a final merry stir or two with a spoon. It's strength was such that it might well have reeked as he poured it out into large cut-glass tumblers, each holding nearly half a pint, but Ma merely said as she sipped at hers:

'Lovely. Just what I wanted. Delicious. One of the best you've ever thought of.'

Pop treated these compliments with airy modesty. It was nothing. One thing he was certain of, though – there was a bit more to it than Lady Violet's sherry.

'Ah! yes, tell me some more about Lady Violet,' Ma said. 'What else did you buy?'

Pop told her about the buggy and Ma said that was nice too. He also told her about the bassinet and Ma said they too were all the rage for putting flowers into nowadays. Then he told her about the little room, the dust, the dusty ginger-nuts, the dead primroses and the staring owl. He knew they would haunt him for a long time.

Finally he told her about the cigar and how he thought

it had made her happy. He didn't expect Ma to laugh about it and he was really glad when she said, half-reproachfully:

'What did you do that for? You've probably gone and made the poor thing bad by this time.'

'She went at it as if it was Christmas pud and turkey,' Pop said. 'Like a meal. I half wish I hadn't done it now.'

He drank deeply at his Moon-Rocket and then filled up the two glasses again.

'Think she'd be offended if I took a bit of grub round when Montgomery and me go to fetch the buggy the day after tomorrow? She looks as if half a puff of wind would blow her away.'

'We've got that big ham in cut,' Ma said. 'And I'm making *Quiche Lorraine* and sausage rolls tomorrow. I'll make a bit of a basket up. By the way, who's your foreign letter from?'

Pop, laughing, his sadness about the morning receding now, said he was damned if he knew. He didn't know anybody in foreign parts. Not a soul.

'Well, open it and see.'

'I'll just mix another jugful first,' Pop said. 'When the ice starts melting it waters it down a lot. Hullo, here comes Charley with Blenheim.

Mr Charlton now appeared from the direction of the house, carrying his baby son in one hand and a large glass of lager beer in the other. Pop delighted in calling his grandson Blenheim; it was such a nice round apple of a name.

'Well, how's Charley boy? And how's my little apple?'

Pop at once started to treat his grandson as if he were a pink rubber ball that had to be frequently bounced about a bit, but Ma instantly made loud noises of remonstration and said the child was only just awake and did Pop want salt water in his drinks or what?

'Give him to me,' she said and Mr Charlton's little son instantly disappeared like a rosy fledgeling into the vast bolster of her bosom, nuzzling eagerly against her. 'And you needn't go in there, young man, either. There's nothing there for you.'

Mr Charlton now found himself staring down at the rose-ringed chamber-pot, which Ma had placed by her camp-stool.

'Oh! you might well look,' Ma said, laughing ripely again. 'That's Pop's present to me. And there's two more.'

Accustomed as he was to living in the Larkin household, Mr Charlton was now never surprised by anything, even by the newest kind of present Pop had decided to give to Ma. He had already seen the pick-up heavily laden with its morning load of junk and even the suits of armour hadn't raised in him the slightest ripple of surprise. He remembered a day when Pop had bought a church organ, fifty-odd pews, about the same number of hassocks, a brass lectern and a pulpit.

He now merely took a calm swig of his beer and gazed with enraptured admiration at Ma's blue interpretation of his wife's bust and then heard Pop say:

'This letter's all in Dutch. Or German or summat. Here, Charley boy, you'd better look at this.'

Mr Charlton took the letter, which was in a neat slanting hand, and looked at it.

'French,' he said, 'not Dutch.'

'It's all Dutch to me,' Pop said. 'Who the pipe's it from?'

Mr Charlton indulged in a short flutter of laughter.

'It seems to be from your old friend,' he said. 'Mademoiselle Dupont.'

'Well, I'll go to Jericho,' Pop said.

'Love letters from France now, eh?' Ma said laughing again. 'What perfume is it soaked in?'

'Well, translate,' Mariette said. 'Let's hear. We're all waiting.'

Mariette had returned from the house less than a minute before, but without little Oscar, who was still asleep. She was now wearing a light purple blouse and rather tight pale green shorts, against which her bare limbs shone like brown butter.

'Well, she first of all presents all her dearest felicitations to the whole Larkin family, from Milord Larkin down to little Oscar. Scarcely a day passes but what she thinks of them and of England. She thinks especially of the milord and the Rolls Royce with the monograms and also the nightingales. She says the nightingales arouse in her an impassioned nostalgia—'

'Good God,' Pop said, 'sounds like some form of asthma.'

'She is bewitched – no, perhaps enchanted is the better word – by the thought – no, the desire, the constant desire – to come to England. The desire, she says, has lately become irresistible and would it any way incom-

mode the Larkin family if she could come soon? Ah!
yes, she goes on – for the special occasion—'

'Special occasion?' Ma said. 'What special occasion?'

Mr Charlton folded up the letter and said in his mild
way that he'd be damned. It wasn't often that he was
damned but this was one time when he clearly was and
he now reminded Ma that they all seemed to have
forgotten something.

'After all you did ask her to be godmother to little
Oscar. I wrote to her myself. And after all one of his
names is Dupont.'

'All right,' Ma said in the blandest possible way, 'what
about it?'

'She wants to come for the christening.'

'Christening?' Pop said, exactly as if this were some
strange, outlandish tribal rite of which he had heard only
very recently. 'Christening? We never said nothing about
no christening, Ma, did we?'

'Not that I can think of.'

'Well, if Ma says we didn't, we didn't, and that's
that. What's he got to be christened for?'

'Well it *is* customary,' Mr Charlton said, with an
irony so faint that it was utterly lost on Pop. 'Well, in
most families anyway. It *is* done.'

'Never?'

'Certainly Mariette and I are going to have Blenheim
done.'

'Never?' Pop seemed astounded, even pained, by
this startling announcement. 'Never had none of ours
done, did we, Ma?'

23

'My God,' Mr Charlton said. 'Not one?'

Mr Charlton for once felt shocked. It was heathenish. It simply wasn't the thing. It had been hard enough for him to get used to the fact that Ma and Pop weren't married and that in painful consequence all the seven children, including his own wife, had been born out of wedlock, but this new discovery was too much.

'But why?' he said. 'Why?'

'Got plenty else to do, hadn't we, Ma?' Pop said and swiftly gave her one of his bolder winks which she returned just as swiftly with a handsome and deliberately seductive smile. 'Eh?'

'Busy as bees,' Ma said. 'I had four in five years once, with the twins.'

'Really never had the time,' Pop said.

Crushingly defeated by this blank, simple statement of historic fact Mr Charlton could only sip at his beer resignedly, saying that anyway even if it was too late to do anything about Montgomery, Mariette, Zinnia, Petunia, Primrose and Victoria they could at least have Oscar and little Blenheim done. That was if Ma and Pop had no objection?

'Oh! no objection at all,' Ma said. 'Any excuse for a party.'

This remark not only made her laugh again but reminded her that it was getting on for lunch time. Pop had better start carving the ham while she put on the potatoes. And if Mariette wanted to help she'd find three melons cut ready on the kitchen table. They were French and a bit expensive but that was all the more reason for having a drop of port in them. There was no sense in buying expensive melons if you were going to be measly about them, was there?

Pop agreed and said in that case they might just as well have port to drink anyway and urged Mr Charlton to go and put a bottle on ice right away. Mr Charlton, quiet now, went into the house, followed by Ma carrying little Blenheim and Pop carrying the chamber-pot, which he now and then struck sharply with his knuckles, so that it gave out a ringing, almost clarion sound.

'Good quality,' he said, 'this 'ere Regency stuff.'

Over large plates of the tenderest ham, princely in flavour – Pop had raised the pig himself – together with new potatoes richly buttered and freckled with fresh parsley, Mr Charlton presently opened a discussion on the question of godparents for the two babies and the eventual date of the christening.

'We shall have to consult the Rev. Spink,' he said, 'and fix a day.'

'Oh! old Frog-face,' Pop said. 'Gawd A'mighty.'

The prospect of the christening, especially by the Reverend Frog-face, began to please him less and less. The Reverend Frog-face struck him as a damned old humbug. Very tall, elderly, cadaverous, onion-skinned and altogether of half-perished appearance, Spink rode aloofly about the village on a bicycle of antique design that had a strange net-work saddle rather like a sagging tennis racquet left out in the rain. Half-intoxicated with popery, Spink intoned Sunday services in Latin, which no one could understand even when they could hear it, which was seldom, with the result that most Sundays there were rather more people in the choir than in the congregation.

A conviction that it was just as good to worship the Lord of creation in a wood of bluebells as in an atmosphere stale with incense and the odour of spent candles had long since struck Pop as being a right and sensible one and now he felt plunged in gloom.

'What about asking Edith Pilchester to be one of the godparents for your little Blenheim?' Ma said. 'That would be a good idea, wouldn't it?'

Mr Charlton said firmly that he couldn't agree. He hated to say it, but Edith was too old. The essence of the thing was that a godparent should be young. Comparatively so, anyway.

'Got anybody in mind?' Ma said.

'Well, as a matter of fact we've already asked Angela Snow.'

Pop instantly perked up as if pricked by a hot pin.

'What did she say?'

'Oh! she was delighted.'

'You never told us,' Pop said. 'You don't suppose she'd act for little Oscar too, do you?'

'It's entirely up to her,' Mr Charlton said. 'If she feels up to the responsibility.'

'I'll ring her up tonight!'

With the gloom on his horizon suddenly largely dispelled, Pop watched with great relish the first strawberries of the year come to the table. They were fat, shining as if enamelled and half-drenched in cream.

Their summeriness suddenly excited all his thoughts about Angela. It would be good to sort of have her in the family. She was still as sensationally beautiful as ever and he couldn't help thinking that it was, after all, a good thing she hadn't married the Brigadier. It was the sensible thing; now they were just good friends. The Brigadier had rightly decided that he was too old for her and it didn't seem right, as Pop had often remarked to Ma, to cramp her style.

'Well, I must be off,' he said, after a third plate of strawberries and another glass or two of port. 'I think I know where I can lay hands on a nice little pie-bald for the buggy.'

'Buggy?' Mariette said. 'What buggy?'

'Pop's bought a nice little buggy from Lady Violet this morning,' Ma said.

'I thought it would be nice for Oscar and little Blenheim to have rides in,' Pop explained. 'Round and round the meadow, so they wouldn't get run over.'

'Oh! Pop,' Mariette said, 'you still think of the nicest things,' and suddenly gave him one of those full-mouthed generous kisses that always reminded him so powerfully of Ma in the prime of her youth.

Out in the garden, in the hot sun, a combination of the rich calling of birds, the smell of earth warmed and grass juicily rising and finally the sight of Ma's canvas, stool and easel inspired him to remember Mariette posing in the never-never and also the idea that he too, perhaps, might yet take up the painting lark.

That, he thought, would be the day.

3

Two days later the morning was so beautiful, drenched with all the full essence of summer, that Pop decided to walk the pie-bald pony over to Lady Violet's bungalow himself, leaving Montgomery to feed turkeys, hens, guinea fowl, pigs, geese, cats and anything else that might need nourishment about the junk-yard. It was only a mile away.

He felt wonderfully calm and at peace with the world. He thought the pony was very pretty with its cocoa and cream markings and the idea had already occurred to him that he ought to try and lay his hands on a couple of silver bells for the harness, one to be engraved Oscar and the other Blenheim, so that there would be a smart old jingling as pony and buggy jogged along. The children were going to call the pony Blossom and the only thing that worried him at all was whether it would be man enough to draw Ma, if and when the occasion arose.

He was surprised, at the bungalow, to see a thinnish, straight-haired woman of forty or so on her hands and knees in the middle of the garden path, armed with an ancient pair of scissors, prising up weeds. Her face, yellowish in colour, looked very like a deflated chamois leather bag. Her stony eyes were depressingly neutral in colour and they seemed to jump, as if frightened, when he greeted her.

'Morning. Beautiful morning. Lady Violet in?'

'I'm awfully afraid she isn't up yet. She isn't feeling very well.' She darted nervous glances towards the bungalow. 'I'll call my husband.'

She at once fluttered desperately back up the garden path, to be met on the threshold of the bungalow by an ebullient man, beer-faced and with a walnut-brown, well-kept moustache, dressed in a thick red flannel shirt, a yellow tie and green linen trousers.

'For Jesus Christ's sake, woman, why must you always run? Don't run everywhere! I've told you a million times.'

'There's a gentleman – a man—'

'All right, all right. He won't *eat* you, will he?'

The man advanced heavily down the garden path, periodically grooming his moustache with elaborate strokes of his hand.

'Morning, morning,' Pop said. 'Larkin's the name. Nice morning.'

'I'm Captain Broadbent. What can I do for you?'

Pop explained about the buggy. The Captain's voice was coarse. His manner was florid and set Pop on edge. The too-often repeated habit of grooming the too-handsome moustache not only irritated him but even made him, a rare thing for him, slightly ill-tempered.

'Ah! you're the johnny who buys junk. I've heard of you.'

Pop so highly resented being called a johnny that he

found himself, with amazement, resisting an unusual and powerful impulse to knock the Captain down. His good nature saved him, however, and he merely walked away.

The Captain followed. Pop untied the pie-bald where he had left him by the garden fence. The Captain gave the pony a brief look of undisguised contempt and said something about the untutored animal not getting very far in the Derby, laughing at the same time. Pop decided to ignore the joke and walked across to the wood-shed, where the buggy stood.

'You're never going to ride about in that damned contraption, are you? It's murder.'

Pop, in silence, started to back the pie-bald into the buggy shafts and the Captain laughed again.

'Well, I suppose it's one way of amusing yourself in this bloody awful countryside. God, what a hole. How anybody possibly sticks it out I'm damned if I know.'

'We manage somehow.'

Having heard his beloved countryside befouled Pop felt that he was ready for anything and started, again in silence, to buckle up the harness.

'Even the one and only pub's a bloody mausoleum. At nine o'clock last night there was one cock-eyed yokel in there with the twitch and two fat old trouts who never said a word. What do you do with all the women round here? Lock the poor bitches up in purdah?'

'Oh! there's a tidy bit o' talent about if you know where to look for it.'

'Is there indeed? Tell me where?'

30

Pop, not answering and not really wanting to listen either, stood dreamily buckling the harness, silently dwelling on the attractions of Ma, Mariette, Primrose and the rest of his daughters. He thought also of Angela Snow, whom he had tried to telephone the previous evening about the christening, but without success. The idea of the christening, largely because of Angela, no longer depressed him. All seemed to be going well. Mademoiselle Dupont had already been written to and Ma and Mariette were already up in London, buying Blenheim's christening robe. It seemed as if the date would be the last Sunday in July and it would be a good excuse, as Ma said, for a party.

'I'll lay you a fiver to a boiled egg that if you held a beauty-contest here there wouldn't be a piece of tender meat among the lot. They breed 'em coarse here, like the cattle.'

From a sudden pained recollection of the stony-eyed woman weeding the garden path Pop's mind abruptly leapt, in a moment of inspired vision, to a thought of someone else. Unable to explain why, he was suddenly thinking of a girl named Jasmine Brown. He had been introduced to Miss Brown in a beer-tent at a point-to-point meeting at Easter and had talked to her for a few convulsive moments before someone had whisked her away.

Miss Brown was unforgettable. In her own particular way she out-rivalled Angela Snow. Whereas Angela was all golden, languid and as smooth as honey, Miss Brown was a very dark, smouldering, big-built girl who had matured at twenty into the full-blown mould of a woman ten years older. She was the sort of girl who in a most sensational way radiated heat while remaining, apparently, surprisingly cool herself. She had managed to get him, in Ma's words, properly on the boil.

This inspiring recollection, following so close on the depressing remembrance of the Captain's wife fearfully scraping up weeds, made him first thoughtful and then, in a quiet way, good-humoured again.

'Sorry you don't think much of our girls. You ought to come over to my place sometime.'

The Captain preened his moustache with superior strokes from the back of his right hand.

'Why? You keep a harem or something?'

Pop laughed, stooping down at the same time to buckle the pony's belly-band.

'Well, it looks a bit like that some Sunday afternoons with all of 'em prancing in and out of the swimming pool.'

'Ah! you've fallen for the new status symbol.'

Pop said he didn't know about status symbol. He'd got the pool for swimming in. For fun.

'Junk trade must be flourishing.'

Well, it was fair, Pop admitted, striving hard not to lose his temper again. It was fair.

Suddenly he remembered something else. Ma had decided at the last moment that it really wasn't very nice to send Lady Violet a gift of ham and sausage rolls. It might seem to imply that a titled lady couldn't afford food or was starving or about to go on National Assistance or something of that lark. She thought it would be more tactful to send a bottle of her own cherry brandy. It was very powerful stuff, the cherry brandy.

'I'm sorry to hear Lady Violet ain't all that grand,' Pop said. He privately hoped it wasn't the cigar. Perhaps it was a bit rash, after all, the cigar. Still – 'I've got a little present for her. I just remembered.'

Before tying up the pony he had put the bottle of cherry brandy under the seat of the buggy and he now leaned over to fetch it out.

'By Jove, a bottle, eh? What's this, what's this?'

'Cherry brandy. Morella. Ma's special. Seven years in bottle.'

'By God, this'll make the day.'

'And when I say brandy I mean brandy. None of your muck. Napoleon V.S.O.P.'

The Captain, for a moment shedding arrogance, seemed to become positively friendly. In an unguarded moment he actually addressed Pop as 'old boy'.

'Ma does peach and apricot too,' Pop said. 'You know where my place is? Drop in and have a nip sometime.'

Was this an invitation? the Captain wanted to know.

Pop, who tried to find some good in everybody, even the worst of stinkers, outsiders and the rest, said in his customary expansive fashion that of course it was.

'Drop in next Sunday afternoon and have a swim. We'll have a party going by about three.'

'Sounds damn' tempting. Harem and all?'

Pop laughed, at the same time reflectively stroking the pony's mane, and said he'd do his best to find a few

33

good hand-picked ones and then added, in his blandest fashion:

'Course, I know you're not narrow-minded or anything. Man of the world and all that. But don't be surprised if you see one or two of 'em running round in the never-never.'

'The girls? Good God.'

Airily Pop explained about Ma and the painting lark and anyhow the Captain must know how it was these days. Everybody free and easy and all that. Nobody capable of being shocked by nothing no more.

He didn't know about that, the Captain had to confess. There were after all limits. He suddenly seemed rather stiff, poised somewhere between pained surprise and curiosity. For a few seconds he positively scrubbed his moustache with a hand so nervously eager to demonstrate a dignified superiority that it was almost priggish.

'Well, I shall have to see how I'm fixed. Very kind of you and all that, Larkin—'

'Here, dammit,' Pop said, 'if I'm going to all the trouble to hand-pick 'em for you and when I tell 'em you'll be there—' the Captain fell to preening his moustache with a now gentler hand – 'you twig what I mean? And after all they'll all be nice girls. Five of 'em my daughters. Just a family party with a few more thrown in. There's be some pretty good snifters too.'

At the thought of snifters the Captain became suddenly amiable again. Well, he expected he'd be there all right. He'd got to relieve the bloody tedium somehow. He glanced with significance towards the bungalow and

Pop, silent again, seemed once again to see the fragile figure of Lady Violet and the fearful hunted figure of the wife fumbling among the weeds.

'About three on Sunday then. Perfick! Let's hope it's a good sweltering hot day. Some of the girls are trying to get brown all over.'

A moment later he was in the buggy, waving an abrupt farewell and driving away. The pony trotted well, he thought; it seemed quite at home in the buggy. It seemed as aware as any human being of the bright pristine beauty of the summer morning and now and then gave an excited snorting sniff with its nostrils, as if drinking at the scent of bluebells, growing grass and may.

Pop breathed hard at them too. The air was cleaner now. The only blemish on the face of the morning was the picture of the Captain's wife among her weeds and somehow he couldn't get that yellow, fearful, fumbling figure out of his mind.

4

Late that evening, after admiring for the eighth or ninth time since supper the suits of armour, the shields and the battle-axes in the passage – there was no doubt that they gave the place terrific tone, terrific – Pop called Angela Snow on the telephone. Her voice, drawling, aristocratic and bewitching as ever, reproached him in tones of languid honey.

'I hate you, sweetie. I don't love you any more. You abandon me for weeks on end.'

Laughing, Pop was quick to assure her with a honied affection of his own that she was, on the contrary, for ever in his thoughts.

'In, yes,' she said, 'and out again. You must want something badly, sweetie, or you'd never ring me.'

Pop blandly confessed that he did indeed want something. In fact, two things.

'Greedy wretch. What's the first?'

When Pop explained about the christening she made purring noises at the other end of the line, assuring him of her undying devotion to himself, Ma and little Oscar. She was even ready, she declared, to be godmother to all his children if need arose and Pop was on the point of saying that it might well do at that when she said:

'Well, and what was the other?'

The other, Pop said, wasn't so easy. It was about a girl.

'You cad. You serpent. You stinking traitor.'

'I just wondered if you knew her, that's all.'

'If I do I shall promptly wring her neck. And yours into the bargain, sweetie.'

'Well, if it's like that,' Pop said, 'I'd better hang up, hadn't I?'

'You do and I'll never forgive you. Who is this Venus you're after? Won't I do instead?'

'Her name's Jasmine Brown. Know her? I met her—'

'Dearest Jasmine. Of course I know her. We graduated through virginity together.'

These remarks were exactly the sort of thing that endeared Angela Snow very deeply to Pop. She was his sort all right, he told himself, laughing with quiet satisfaction. It might even be, he hoped, that Jasmine Brown was his sort too.

'Are you still there, sweetie?' Angela Snow said. 'You make me very suspicious. What do you want with Jasmine?'

'I just wondered if you'd like to bring her over for a swim on Sunday.'

'What a piffling excuse. You make me more suspicious than ever. She's blisteringly attractive, this girl. As if you didn't know.'

'No, honest,' Pop said. 'I'm just trying to make up a good party. Got to get some good scenery, after all. There's a feller named Broadbent coming along. Captain Broadbent—'

'Oh! my God, not that one.'

'So you know him too?'

'Met him once at a party, sweetie. Which was quite enough.'

'Stinker?' Pop said.

'The great self-styled lady-killer of all time, I gather.'

Pop laughed loudly, so that the sound crackled joyously in Angela Snow's ear, making her say:

'I'm still awfully suspicious, sweetie. I can't help thinking you're up to something. You're not by any chance thinking of sacrificing Jasmine and me on the Broadbent altar, are you?'

'Good Gawd, no,' Pop said.

'I'm profoundly glad to hear it, sweetie. We're sporting girls, but not that sporting. I gather he's already been thrown out of every club and hunt in the county.'

Pop positively barked with delight into the telephone.

'It was somethink like that,' he said, 'that I'd got in mind.'

'You don't mean it? Charming. Absolutely charming.'

Pop didn't say a word for another moment or two. He didn't want to do anything indelicate, he thought, and he found his next sentence for once rather a difficult one to phrase.

'Is she the real sport?' he said. 'Jasmine, I mean?'

'My dear, she's the most uninhibited creature on God's earth.'

'Unin – what?'

Pop, continually eager though he was to broaden his education by television and such means, now and then still came up against another long word that had him floored.

'I mean she's like me only more so. She's the sort of girl who goes to a shop to try on a new dress, sheds all and doesn't bother to pull the cubicle curtains.'

This delicious picture of the wholly uninhibited Miss Brown set Pop chuckling warmly. This was the stuff, absolutely perfick, he was about to tell her when she said:

'The nice thing is that she's got brains too. Just give her a bare hint of what's expected of her and she'll—'

'Bare it might be an' all,' Pop said darkly, chuckling again. 'Anyway bring her to lunch. I'll get Ma to do a turkey. I've got a new lot o' sparkling red burgundy – I'll get it nice and cold. Must go now. Ma's gone up to bed already. Good-bye. Bless you. Love.'

'Farewell, dear man. Fondest love. We'll be there.'

When Pop finally went upstairs ten minutes later it was to find Ma still sitting at her dressing table, brushing her thick dark hair with a silver brush half as big as a tennis racquet and wearing a bright magenta nightgown so short in style that it merely covered little more than the top half of her huge cushiony body like a parasol.

'Been having a long chin-wag with somebody, haven't you?' she said. 'Who was it?'

'Angela. Been inviting her and one of her girl friends over for a swim on Sunday. Girl named Jasmine Brown.'

'Nice one?'

Pop, laughing richly, proceeded to explain to Ma about Miss Brown's entire lack of inhibition, careful at the same time not to use the exact word in case Ma shouldn't be any more familiar with it than he was.

'Sounds just your type,' Ma said, laughing too.

Pop said he hoped so; he was looking forward to it a lot.

'Very glad to hear it,' Ma said. 'You've been a bit quiet lately. I'd almost begun to think you'd gone off the boil.'

Pop freely admitted he'd been quiet but not by any means off the boil: not on your nelly.

'Something on your mind?' Ma said. 'You'd better get it off your chest if there is.'

Pop said as a matter of fact there was and proceeded to tell her about Lady Violet's niece, Mrs Broadbent, and how he hadn't been able to get that crushed, haunted, groping figure out of his mind all day.

'She looked as if she'd been horse-whipped,' he said. 'Who by?'

Pop, standing at the foot of the bed, taking off his collar and tie, explained about the Captain, his distasteful contempt for local ladies, his arrogance about Pop's beloved countryside and how, it seemed, he was the self-styled ladykiller of all time.

'Sounds *most* attractive. What did you tell him?'

'I invited him over for a swim on Sunday.'

'Well, that's a fine thing. Are you mad? Do you want the pool contaminated or something?'

'No, no. I just thought he ought to meet a few real ladies, that's all. Like Angela and Jasmine Brown.'

'Oh! it's like that, is it?'

Pop, laughing, said it was, or somethink of that sort. Ma, who had now finished brushing her hair, started drenching her great bosom with Chanel No. 5, shaking it from what seemed to be a quart-size bottle. As she did so she thought of Angela Snow. What had she said, Ma wondered, about the idea of being god-mother?

'Thrilled to bits.'

'That was nice of her. That reminds me – the parson telephoned. He'll be round tomorrow evening to fix up about the christening.'

'Frog-face, eh?'

No, Ma said, it wasn't Frog-face. It was a young man – a locum or whatever it was they called them. Frog-face was away sick – having an operation for gall-stones or something nasty.

Pop said he was sorry to hear that and wondered if he ought not to take some sort of nourishment, prefer-ably liquid, into the patient? A bottle of vodka, perhaps? It might dissolve the stones.

'They say they do dissolve them nowadays,' Ma said. 'Anyway he won't be well enough for the christening, that's sure.'

'We'll make a marvellous do of it, that day, Ma. We'll really light up.'

'I should think so too,' Ma said. 'After all we've never had a christening in the family before.'

The following evening a young man of earnest demeanour, pale ginger-haired hands, scrubby, carroty hair and a voice that ended all its hesitant sentences with an almost musical squeak, like that of dry leather, sat in a state of stupefied bewilderment in the sitting room, utterly unable to reconcile Pop's chromium galleon of a cocktail cabinet with the baronial armour regaling the passage outside or the luscious graces of Primrose and Mariette with the bucolic comradeship of Pop, who frequently called him 'Mr Candy, old man' and had, in response to a mild request for 'just a little whisky please', given him three-quarters of a tumblerful, neat except for a couple of cubes of ice and the merest teaspoon of water.

Mariette and Primrose having been introduced as 'two of my daughters, not the ones to be christened, though' and Primrose more especially as 'the intellectual one of the family, sort of. Likes poetry', Mr Candy sat in a state of twitching suspense, enmeshed as a fly in a spider web by the rapturous beauty of Primrose, now, at fourteen, as fully developed as a woman of twenty and every bit as well aware of it too. Her dark eyes dwelt on Mr Candy with open insistence, bringing his face out in a repeated tepid blush.

After Pop had apologised for the absence of Mr Charlton, who had gone out to take a trial run in a second-hand Jaguar that Pop had just taken over in a deal, Mr Candy said:

'Oh! I'm sorry I shall miss him. He of course is the father of the two children who are to be christened?'

'Oh! no,' Pop said. 'He's the father of one and I'm the father of the other.'

'I see. Son and grandson. Rather unique.'

'You can't say "rather unique",' Primrose said, gazing at Mr Candy with almost fervent remonstration. 'It's either unique or it isn't.'

Mr Candy, the hairs on whose head and hands actually seemed to redden even deeper as the blood rushed to his skin, admitted that of course you couldn't. It was silly of him. He ought to have known better.

'Clever girl, our Primrose,' Pop said. 'You can't get over Primrose.'

Mr Candy, acutely embarrassed, started fumbling in his inside jacket pocket for pen and paper. As he did so his dog collar went slightly askew, cutting against his Adam's apple, which stuck out prominently from his rather scraggy neck. This caused Ma to think that perhaps he was another one of those who didn't get enough to eat and inquired with earnest solicitude if he wouldn't like a piece of pork pie?

'Oh! no, no, no. Thanks all the same. I really wouldn't.'

'Well, I would,' Pop said. 'Good idea.'

'I'll get it,' Primrose said.

'And bring the ketchup,' Pop said.

Before Primrose came back with a pork-pie a quarter cut, a bottle of tomato ketchup and several knives and plates the Rev. Candy said:

'And now may I have the names of the two children? I always like to make sure of the spellings and so on.'

'Well,' Ma said, 'Oscar – that's ours – is going to be called Oscar Columbus Septimus Dupont Larkin.'

Mr Candy, who seriously thought for one painful moment that he must be having his leg pulled, flushed deeply again and seized on the word Septimus, inquiring:

'Septimus. The seventh? You have seven children?'

'Think so,' Ma said, laughing richly. 'Lose count a bit sometimes. What with little Blenheim and everything.'

'Blenheim?' Mr Candy said. 'Blenheim?'

'Oh! he's the other one,' Ma said. 'Mariette's baby. He's going to be called John Churchill Marlborough Blenheim Charlton.'

'Great Heavens.'

'Something wrong?' Ma inquired.

It was nothing, Mr Candy said, so embarrassed again that he actually answered Pop's enthusiastic 'Have a piece of pie, old man? Very good. Ma's own make', with an unexpected yes, after all, he thought he would.

Primrose cut the pie with her own hands, placing a big wedge of it on a plate, with a knife, in front of Mr Candy, at the same time inquiring if he wouldn't like ketchup? Mr Candy, who was desperately trying to write down the names of Mariette's baby correctly and in correct order, said he didn't think he would and took a strong gulp of whisky.

Pop, who was dipping his own piece of pie with great relish into a large red pool of ketchup, then remarked that Ma had painted a very nice picture of Blenheim and Mariette the other day. Perhaps Mr Candy would like to see it?

Mr Candy said he would. 'It seems everyone is taking

up painting nowadays. My mother paints. Mostly flowers.'

'Go and fetch the picture, Primrose,' Ma said, 'there's a dear. It's on the top of the fridge.'

Two minutes later Mr Candy, abruptly pausing in the act of putting a piece of pork pie into his mouth, found himself gazing at a picture of Mariette entirely in the nude except for a narrow glimpse of the purple briefs. The baby was asleep slightly to the side of one splendid breast. Ma had been for some time very exercised about the purple briefs, not knowing whether to paint them in or not, in case they might not be understood. Now she thought they looked very nice – and art, she had read somewhere, had to be honest if it was to be anything at all – especially against Mariette's skin, which she had on this occasion painted the deep gold colour of a ripe pumpkin.

'Think it's anything like her, Mr Candy?' Pop inquired with a sort of brisk innocence.

Mr Candy, unacquainted as he was with the sitter, or at least those parts of her so boldly depicted by Ma, was simply crushed to silence, redder than ever. A trembling cube of pork pie jelly stuck to his open lips, faltered there for a few moments and then went bouncing down his black clerical front, from which Mr Candy at last retrieved it with fumbling fingers.

'Well, anyway, Ma, I'll tell you this,' Pop said, 'I like 'em better now you've done 'em that gold colour instead of blue.'

Well, they did look more real, certainly, Ma admitted.

'You're getting better at it, that's what it is, Ma.

More experienced,' Pop said. 'I tell you what – you ought to do a big family group one of these days.'

Mr Candy was saved from any further discussion of this interesting possibility by the sudden entry of the twins, Zinnia and Petunia, each wearing bright scarlet bathing wraps and sucking iced lollies of a sort of pistachio green shade. Ma, having introduced them by name to Mr Candy, then introduced Mr Candy in turn as the gentleman who was going to christen Oscar and little Blenheim.

Simultaneously the twins demanded in shrill voices to know why they couldn't be christened too? They hadn't ever been done, had they?

Profoundly shocked, a piece of pork pie poised at his lips, Mr Candy said he most fervently hoped so.

'Surely, Mrs Larkin?'

'Afraid not,' Ma said.

'Great Heavens, what an extraordinary omission.'

In tones of velvet wonder Primrose now inquired what about her?

'Good Lord,' she said, giving Mr Candy the most provocative of luscious looks, 'haven't I been christened either? I can't wait!'

Mr Candy, held by the precocious, luscious eyes, felt he couldn't wait either. He desperately wanted to flee. It would have been merciful if he could have hidden himself somewhere. For a moment he half-choked on a chunk of pork pie and Ma said:

'You look a bit pale, Mr Candy. Feeling all right?'

'Perfectly. Only it's rather an odd circumstance to find

a whole family of seven that hasn't received baptismal rites.'

'Suppose it is,' Ma admitted, 'but you see Pop and me were too busy at the time getting on with other things.'

'Oh! couldn't we all be done together?' Primrose said. 'We could, Mr Candy, couldn't we? There's no age–limit, is there?'

Unfortunately not, Mr Candy wanted to say but couldn't bring himself even remotely to the point of saying it. In a daze, the sudden victim of open feminine entreaty, he could only say:

'One can receive the baptism at any time.'

'Marvellous,' Primrose said. 'Absolutely marvellous. Let's all be done together.'

'Cheaper by the dozen, I suppose?' Pop said. 'Drop more whisky, Mr Candy?'

'No, no, no. Really not, thank you.'

'Go on, old man. Drink up. You'll need it. After all you've got a lot more work on your hands than you bargained for, haven't you?'

He had indeed, Mr Candy thought, he had indeed. If one could call it that.

Silent again, he watched Pop replenish his already generous measure of whisky, Pop at the same time inquiring if Mr Candy couldn't find room for the other bit of pork pie? Mr Candy protested, though not very strongly, that he couldn't and was pained and astonished a moment later to hear the seductive voice of Primrose entreating:

'Go on, Mr Candy, share it with me. Half and half. You and I share.'

With unresisting eyes Mr Candy wretchedly watched her cut the remains of the pork pie in half and then with a deliberately over-delicate gesture put the larger portion on his plate. The moment was one of such intimacy that for the next few seconds he was mesmerised into thinking that she and Mariette, so alike in their dark beauty, had become interchanged. The golden bust seemed to mature into palpitating reality before his eyes.

'I love pork pie, don't you?' she said, in tones also golden, so that she might actually have been inviting him to accept some rare physical favour.

There was no doubt that people were right when they said girls grew up fast these days, Mr Candy thought. They certainly did; they were women before they started, he told himself, and for one awful moment had a vision of himself in church, painfully enacting the ritual of baptism for one beautiful Larkin after another.

'Oh! I'm absolutely thrilled,' Primrose said. 'I can't wait for that Sunday. We'll all have new dresses, won't we, Ma?'

'Course,' Ma said. 'You don't think we're going to turn out in sack-cloth and ashes do you?'

Pop was also moved to express his thrill and pride. He was blowed if it wouldn't be quite something to see his whole brood being sprinkled at one go, little Blenheim an' all.

Fortified by a further gulp of whisky Mr Candy was impelled to remind Pop that the occasion was one of great solemnity.

'Course,' Pop said. 'Course. Pardon me.'

'If you don't mind my saying so your attitude ought to be one of "better late than never".'

'We'll see it doesn't happen again,' Ma said.

Pop couldn't help wondering what Ma meant by that exactly. You could take it two ways.

'Well, shall we settle on the day?' Mr Candy said. He felt again that it was time to go. The over-generous measure of whisky was putting a slight slur on his speech and the already warm June evening seemed to be growing rapidly more and more stifling. 'You did suggest the third Sunday in July?'

'That's right,' Ma said.

'And there will be how many for baptism? Seven?'

'Eight,' Ma said. 'Three boys and five girls.'

The Lord give him strength and patience, Mr Candy felt himself silently entreating.

'Eight,' Pop said. 'That's set me back a shillin' or two.'

Mr Candy pointed out that there was, on the contrary, no charge for the service. But of course a contribution—

'Leave that to me,' Pop said in his most generous fashion, 'leave that to me. Nice to know there's a few things left that are free.'

'Yes, isn't it?' Primrose said, again looking Mr Candy straight in the eyes.

Mr Candy felt he could bear no more; this was the signal for departure. He started to get to his feet, succeeded in rising seven or eight inches or so and then fell back again. The act of sitting down in the chair, far from being awkward or embarrassing, was pleasurable. He actually gave a short chuckle.

'Perhaps Mr Candy would like a lift home?' Ma said.

'Be a bit difficult,' Pop said, 'unless I take him in the pick-up. The Rolls has got a flat tyre and Charley ain't back yet.'

'I could take him in the buggy,' Primrose said.

'No, no,' Mr Candy said. 'I shall walk across the meadows, the way I came.'

'Riding in the buggy's absolutely marvellous,' Primrose said. 'We've only just got it.'

'I don't think I've ever ridden in a buggy.'

'No? It's an absolutely wonderful sensation. Quite different from a car. You feel sort of on air.'

'You do?' Mr Candy said and started to get up again, this time succeeding in standing fully erect, so that Pop said:

'You let our Primrose drive you home, Mr Candy. She handles the pie-bald like a real dabster. All my kids are good with horses.'

'That's right,' Ma said. There was something quite attractive about young parsons, she thought, in a moley sort of way. Perhaps it was the collar being wrong way round. 'Well, off you go. Then you can get back before you need the lamps.'

Ten minutes later Mr Candy was sitting in the buggy wrapped in a midsummer dream. Primrose said she would drive by the back lanes; it was quieter that way; there was hardly any traffic. Already Pop had fixed the silver bells to the harness and as the buggy jogged along, not very fast, the delicate jingle of them leapt to the height of the thick hornbeams and hawthorns arching across the road and then came as delicately prancing back again.

'Wonderful sensation. Like it?'

'I do, I do.'

'It must have been wonderful in the old days.'

'What must?'

'This. Riding about like this. Not racing everywhere. You can take everything in so much better.'

Mr Candy, now slightly recovering from the effects of the whisky but still in a pleasant daze, agreed. The little pie-bald slowed to a walk and Primrose said:

'You notice that? That's a trick of his. He's very artful. It's to get me to stop on the side of the road and let him graze.'

'Is it indeed?' Mr Candy said. 'Is it?'

'Clever as a monkey, this pony,' Primrose said and a few moments later drew the buggy into the shadow of a big Spanish chestnut, by a gateway. 'You simply let him graze for a few moments and then he's all right again.'

The pony grazed; an occasional solitary tinkle of bell broke on the calm and pellucid air. Many birds were still singing, deepening rather than breaking the silence, and the scent of may was clotted and intoxicating everywhere.

'I'm thrilled that you're going to christen me.'

Primrose spoke in a whisper and Mr Candy sat silent, unable to think of a suitable reply.

'I mean I'm thrilled it's you and not anyone else.'

'Really? Me? Why me?'

'Because you're you and no one else.'

Mr Candy started to feel uncomfortable to the point of trembling. His hands felt hot and clammy. In confusion he started to say something about the act of christening being something into which no hint of personality could or should enter and she said:

'I know all about that. But it'll be different with you. I know.'

All of a sudden Primrose appeared to be holding up her face to be kissed. Mr Candy, recoiling, didn't know whether to resist this in outspoken refusal or clerical reprimand, but Primrose saved him the trouble by putting her soft, moist, partly opened lips on his.

Mr Candy felt himself reel in complete astonishment and then become inert, his lips hard and flat. After about half a minute of this Primrose disengaged herself from the unequal struggle and said:

'You don't encourage people very much, do you?' and in the artless innocence of the question it might well have been Ma speaking.

'I don't think it's proper that I should.'

'Proper, why proper? We're all alone, aren't we?'

'Well, even if I thought it proper I don't think your mother would quite approve.'

'No?' The single word, so palpably innocent as to imply almost nothing at all, was followed by a hint of mischief. 'Perhaps you'd rather talk about poetry or something like that?'

Mr Candy didn't particularly want to talk about poetry either and was about to say so when she gave him a lustrous glance of inquiry and said, her voice very soft:

'Do you know Donne?'

Mr Candy was sorry, but he didn't know a thing about Donne.

'He was a parson like you,' she said. 'You mean you don't know that marvellous, marvellous poem of his that begins '*I wonder by my troth what thou and I did till we loved*'?'

Mr Candy didn't know about that either and excused his ignorance by pointing out that he'd spent a good part of the last three or four years helping out in a parish in the East End of London where, on the whole, he didn't think Donne would cut much ice.

'In the East End? Doing what?'

'Oh! welfare work. Youth clubs and that sort of thing. Rather toughish sometimes. One had to learn to take care of oneself.'

'I'm sorry you don't know about Donne,' she said. 'He puts it all so gorgeously.' She turned and sat full face to him, dark eyes absolutely still, and gave him another glance of such lustrous and captivating quality that he felt the muscles of his throat contracting sharply. 'There's another one that starts '*Dear love, for nothing less than thee would I have broke this happy dream.*' Don't you know that?'

Mr Candy confessed he was absolutely ignorant of that one too.

'Rather like us, sitting here, don't you think? I mean I feel in a dream too and don't want anything to break it.'

It was utter madness, Mr Candy suddenly thought, wildly. It had got to be broken. Here he was, sinking under the seductive power of a girl of fourteen and letting himself go under. It was illegal anyway. It was full of ghastly possibilities. It was like being tempted with ripe fruit. Clearly, like all the rest of the family, she hadn't the shadow of an inhibition in her whole being. You could fairly hear her thinking with the pores of her skin.

'I think I really should go—'

'Oh! don't go. Why? You're not afraid of being alone with me here, are you?'

Oh! no, it wasn't that he was afraid—

'What then?'

Well, it was just that there were – well, to put it frankly, certain limits beyond which – well, you couldn't be involved.

'Oh! are there?'

'Of course there are.'

'Well, it doesn't worry me. I'm doing the involving.'

With irresistible fingers she touched his face. Every pore in Mr Candy's own skin responded in a protest that was also, against all his better nature, as physically pleasurable as the eating of ripe fruit. There was a faint but detectable scent of honey on her lips and a moment later her arms were completely round him and she was giving him a kiss of such protracted, accomplished and passionate nature that he fell back flat against

54

the cushions of the buggy, her young body pressing full against him.

Oh! God, O! God, was all Mr Candy could think, He was sunk; he was in for it now. And how in the name of all the saints was he ever going to get through that awful, awful Sunday?

5

Over-smartly dressed in a light blue suit, sugar-pink shirt, blue and white tie and white buckskin shoes, a dandified curl in both his moustache and hair, Captain Broadbent arrived at the Larkin house about half past three on the following Sunday afternoon. The weather, as Pop had hoped it would be, was hot and the junk-yard a dozy dormitory of prostrate pigs, soporific geese, hens, turkeys and guinea-fowl all resting in the shade of ruined bits of machinery, elder trees and haystacks. Pop's yellow and black Rolls Royce stood under a corrugated hovel and the new Jaguar, a discreet dove-grey, in the shade of a willow tree whose gently turning leaves provided almost the only movement in the summer air.

Outside the front door of the house, to Captain Broadbent's astonishment, stood the two suits of armour, each now nursing a battle-axe in its arms. Ma had decided after all that the inside passage was slightly cramped for them, especially after she had run sharply into them in the twilight one evening. She thought that if anything they looked even more classy outside than in and Pop was inclined to agree with her, especially at night, when he was able to switch on the red, yellow and blue fairy lights inside the vizors.

Walking round to the back of the house, Captain

Broadbent presently found himself facing a scene that merely served to increase the contemptuous astonishment already aroused by junk, armour and general farmyard menagerie. People simply didn't live like this; it just wasn't done. The big swimming pool, its depth a brilliant turquoise blue, was almost indecent in its ostentation, a blown-up status symbol if ever there was one. The screaming of many children reminded him of one of those awful day trips to the seaside. More astonishing than anything else, perhaps, was the fact that Pop, in anticipation of Mademoiselle Dupont's visit from France, had already run up the tricolor on one side of the top diving board, with the Union Jack on the other. Ma had badly wanted to fly the Royal Standard too, but Montgomery had pointed out that you couldn't do that unless the Queen was in residence, which wasn't likely to be yet. Ma, a fervent royalist, said more was the pity.

Half way along one side of the pool Ma, in a bright canary yellow bathing costume, gave the impression of a large well-filled balloon that had ever so gently descended from space and was now resting on the tiniest of camp stools. She was painting on a really large canvas today, trying to embrace the entire pool, tricolor Union Jack, gambolling figures and all.

On the opposite side of the pool was erected a piece of apparatus the like of which Captain Broadbent couldn't ever remember seeing before. It beat the band, he told himself, for sheer vulgarity. He supposed the thing was some sort of portable drink-wagon or bar. The entire affair was made of bamboo, with a roof of palm thatch and designs of coconut and pineapple scratched about it in dark poker-work, so that the whole had a marked Polynesian effect. It was set about with glasses of all colours, emerald, vermilion, purple, amber and blue, together with corkscrews, bottle-openers as big as horse-shoes and scores of bottles and siphons of different kinds. It looked like something out of some beastly opera, Captain Broadbent thought.

He was just on the point of turning his back on this second and even louder symbol of status when Pop, with splendid warmth, hailed him from behind the bar, shaking a vast silver cocktail shaker as his signal of welcome.

'Ah! there you are, Colonel. Didn't think you'd been able to find us. Perfick day, Colonel, eh?'

More by instinct than design Pop was always inclined to promote a military man if he could. In return Captain Boadbent seemed to preen himself at this sudden rise in rank and at once went through the ritual of brushing his moustache with an extravagant sweep of his hand.

'Afternoon, Larkin. Not too early, I trust?'

'Just right, Colonel. Perfick. Come and meet the family. Ma!' he yelled across the pool, 'Colonel Broadbent's just arrived. Colonel, this is Ma. Recently taken up the painting lark. Mostly goes in for the nude.'

'Afternoon, Colonel,' Ma shouted. 'Sweatin' hot, isn't it?'

The Captain, in the middle of the stiffest of bows, slightly recoiled at this description of the day and Pop at once proceeded to introduce the rest of his family.

'Zinnia, Petunia, Montgomery, Victoria – where's Victoria? Oh! that's her, in the red bikini, floating. And Primrose – that's Primrose, just taking the umbrella to Ma. Ma's finding it a bit too hot I fancy. Hope she won't get one of her turns.'

Ma sometimes had turns when it was over-hot and it was a bit of a job sometimes to get her round. Rum generally helped, though.

'And this is my eldest, Mariette. Mrs Charlton. I think Mr Charlton must be having a lay-down indoors somewhere. Unless he's larking about somewhere with the girls.'

As he said this Pop gave the Captain the most indiscreet and knowing of winks, as if the two of them shared some very saucy secret. The Captain hardly knew what to do in return. The young goddess in her dark green bikini, swinging her body along the far side of the pool, a black umbrella twirling over one shoulder, had already unnerved him, so much so that he was totally unprepared to deal with the vision of a three parts naked Mariette, now turning over on her back on a bright blue foam mattress, her breasts every bit as eloquent as her dark eyes as she raised them to the sun.

'Hullo, Colonel,' she said softly, smiling. 'You chose a good day to come,' and it was almost as if she had conferred the promotion on him herself, so that he felt he would surrender his rise in rank only with extreme reluctance, if he surrendered it at all.

'Snifter, Colonel? What'll it be?'

'Something soft and cold, I think, if—'

'Just mixing a new one up,' Pop said. 'Moon-Rocket. Pretty harmless. Mostly ice – dash o' vodka and all that, for flavour. Care to try it? It's a good quencher.'

The Captain, still unnerved and slightly aloof, said he would and Pop made athletic manoeuvres with the cocktail shaker.

'What price our little paradise, Colonel, eh?'

The Captain remained mute; he could put no price on the little paradise at all.

'Well, here we are, Colonel. Try that for size.'

Pop now handed the Captain a tall, silver-rimmed glass that seemed to contain about a pint of amber liquid topped by a sprig of mint, a slice of orange and a cherry. The glass was beautifully frosted and the Captain raised it to his lips at first with caution, then decided it seemed aromatically pleasant and drank deep.

Some twenty seconds later he found himself going through the alarming experience of supposing that he had been electrocuted somewhere in the pit of his stomach. He choked, fighting vainly to regain both equilibrium and breath.

'It's got somethink, Colonel, hasn't it?' Pop said. 'Drink up! Cheers!'

Pop proceeded to lower the level of his own glass by several inches and immediately made as if to fill both glasses up again. The Captain, who was by now convinced that his eyeballs were standing an inch or so out of the top of his head, managed to put his hand over the rim of his glass, at the same time entreating Pop in a much weakened voice to be steady.

Pop, smacking his lips, assured the Captain that this was one of the best he had ever invented. Ma adored it too.

'Ma!' he shouted across the pool, at the same time lifting the cocktail shaker. 'How about you?'

'Please.'

A few minutes later the Captain was assailed by a new vision. It was that of Angela Snow appearing from the direction of the house, tall, elegant and languid as ever, and suddenly he suffered yet another alarming experience: that of supposing she had nothing on. In a moment he remembered Pop's jovial warning to him not to be surprised if he saw some of the girls running round in the never-never and he could only suppose this was some new evidence of vulgarity. Then, as Angela came nearer, he saw that the illusion of nakedness was actually caused by the briefest of bikinis, in colour almost exactly that of her light golden skin. He felt much relieved.

Then as she came nearer still he recognised that he had met her somewhere before: perhaps once or twice at a party. He vaguely recalled that her father was a judge or something of that sort. Anyway she came from the right bloodstock and he couldn't for the life of him think what a well-connected girl like her was doing with this vulgar crowd. He wasn't against democracy and mixing with average chaps and all that but by God there were things which shook you.

'Want you to meet Miss Snow, Colonel. Angela. Very old friend of ours.'

'Colonel?' Angela turned on the Captain the most

bewitching and languid of smiles. 'You were Captain the last time we met. Promoted, eh?'

'Well, I—'

The Captain brushed his moustache, reluctant to deny his sudden rise in rank and Angela said:

'Well, congratulations.'

'Well, actually—'

'Calls for a drink, don't it?' Pop said. 'Angela? What about it? One of my specials?'

'Gorgeous idea.'

The Captain was confused. He preened his moustache with an elliptical sort of sweep, haughtily. He felt uncomfortable and hot. Perhaps, he thought, it was time to get changed? A dip might cool him down.

'Perhaps I might get into some cooler togs, Larkin. Where could I change?'

'In the house,' Pop said. 'I'll come and show you.'

'Jasmine's there,' Angela said and gave Pop a slow, soft, secret wink of her own. 'She'll show the Colonel where.'

'Drink up before you go,' Pop urged the Captain, 'I'll have another ready when you get back,' and the Captain, bracing himself, drank as if at a poison cup.

In a rather shrill voice Ma then called across the pool:

'Why didn't you bring your wife over, Colonel, on a lovely day like this?'

'She doesn't care greatly for the social life, I'm afraid.'

'Oh! don't she? Pity. Wouldn't like me to ring her up and get her over for a cuppa tea, I suppose?'

'I fancy not. She never really stirs out much.'

Once again Pop, as he listened, saw in his mind the image of the fearful, fumbling figure scraping at its weeds.

A moment later little Oscar, chasing a large red-and-blue ball, stumbled awkwardly, fell on his face and lay prostrate, bawling loudly. This was a signal for everyone else to shriek with abandoned laughter, so that the whole afternoon suddenly seemed to explode violently about Captain Broadbent's ears. The din was perfectly maddening and suddenly the Captain, again brushing his moustache, fled from it with what he thought was a certain critical dignity.

The echo of children's caterwauling was still ringing in his ears when he stepped over the Larkin threshold. He supposed he would have to change and get into that filthy pool with all those filthy kids but for a few uncertain moments he found it hard to lower himself to do so. That filthy drink of Larkin's together with the thought of his accidental rise in rank didn't help much either and for a few moments longer he struggled desperately with the idea of whether or not to abandon everything and run.

Two words were enough to extract him from this dilemma and they were spoken so softly that for a moment he was not only uncertain as to where they came from but if they were real at all.

'Hullo there.'

Another feminine vision, this time so stunning as to be almost frightening, stood half way up the stairs. Like something carved out of flawless cream marble, every limb splendidly unblemished, the tall Jasmine Brown leaned voluptuously on the banisters, saved from sheer nakedness only by a trifling arrangement of taut pale green triangles. Even two of these were not enough to cover fully her two deeply assertive breasts, so that the glorious flesh of them stood out half-exposed, in vibrant splendour.

'I'm Jasmine Brown.'

'Oh! yes, they told me – they said something about – you know, you'd show me where to change.'

The Captain moved as if to go up the stairs but to his great consternation Jasmine Brown at that moment decided to sit down plumb in the middle of them, barring his way with legs curved in such a way that, in trying hastily to look away, he gave an undignified stumble and fell up a step or two.

Jasmine Brown laughed softly, in a voice of alarmingly seductive quietness.

'Steady now. You've been having one of those Larkin specials. I know.'

'No, no. I beg your pardon – forgot to introduce myself. Colonel – Captain Broadbent.'

'Colonel or Captain?' she said, in a voice of beautifully modulated inquiry, low and innocent, so that he found it impossible to look her in the face and found himself once again completely mesmerised by her legs, which she had now elegantly drawn up together.

'Colonel,' he half-muttered under his breath, his own voice now so low that it was doubtful if she heard.

'Glorious, those drinks of his.'

'Made me damned hot, if that's anything. I'm dying to get into something cooler.'

'Cool? You look marvellously cool. That's a wonderful suit of yours. I love that colour.'

'Really?'

The Captain, leaning with one hand on the banisters, preened his moustache with the other.

'Stunning. And that shirt and tie. All looks spendidly cool.'

The Captain, though greatly flattered, made as if to advance another step or two upstairs but Jasmine Brown made no sign of moving to help him except to run her hands slowly up and down her legs with a sibilant whisper that was hardly audible even in the profound quietness of the summer afternoon.

'You look so awkward standing there. Why don't you sit down a minute? Come on.' She patted the stair just below her calves. 'Sit.'

'I really ought to go and change—'

'Oh! sit down. There's oceans of time.'

'I suppose so, but – well, one ought to play ball and all that. Not that I particularly want to swim—'

'No. Why not?'

'Damn bedlam out there. It's like some ruddy awful circus. You can't hear yourself think.'

'And who,' she said, again in that voice of lilting innocence, 'wants to think on an afternoon like this? Not this girl, I'll tell you. Come on, sit down.'

The Captain, who had held out firmly until this moment, now sat down on the stairs, only to find in the very same moment that she had slipped her body down one step nearer his.

In this increasingly intimate situation, not knowing what else to say, he bluffed:

'I don't mind telling you I damn nearly ran just now.'

'Not from me I hope?'

'No, no, of course not. From that rabble—'

'If all I hear about you is true the last things you run from are women.'

'Oh? Oh?' he said with a hint of dark inquiry. 'Who's been telling you this?'

'Oh! friends.'

'Friends, eh? Men or women?'

'Both. I understand you make all the men blisteringly jealous and all the women, well—'

Bathed in intoxicating waves of flattery, the Captain could only murmur something about so that's what they said, did they? Well, he supposed he'd had his moments—

'I'll bet you have. And still will, I hope.'

With an increasing uneasiness the Captain found himself caught full in Jasmine's Brown's deep, dark stare. Her large black eyes, liquid and hypnotic, held him relentlessly imprisoned for fully half a minute until in desperation he suddenly released himself and lowered his own eyes, only to find himself facing, a mere fifteen inches away, the full glory of her breasts, which seemed to rise and fall in invitation.

'You know, I honestly ought to go and change—'

'Don't change. I love you in that suit. I really do. Stay here.'

The Captain again preened his moustache but nevertheless felt bound to point out that Larkin would be wondering where the hell he'd got to and after all there were the ethics of the damn' thing. He, the Captain, was after all a guest.

'Oh! the Larkins never worry about things like that. Guests can do what they like here. Disappear to the woods. Play hide and seek. Sit on stairs. Any old thing. It's all free and easy. You know of course that they're not married?'

'Good God.'

'And that none of their children have ever been christened? A great scream, that – they're going to have them all done next month. Wholesale.'

'Are they, by Jove?'

This stupefied reaction expressed not only the Captain's affront at the extraordinary habits of the Larkins but his own rising embarrassment at yet another move of her body. Her warm naked shoulder actually brushed against him as she tossed back her dark hair, no less glorious than the rest of her, so that he actually averted his face.

'I love sitting on stairs and talking, don't you?' she said.

The Captain, suddenly overheated again, felt he would have given anything for a breath of air. It was getting pretty stifling. With discomfort he fidgeted on the stairs but all the encouragement she gave him was another long, bewitching stare, accompanied by the prettiest and most lustrous of smiles, her lips gently pursing and slightly pouting.

'You know, I honestly think you're trying to escape from me,' she said, 'aren't you?'

'Oh! no, no, no.'

'Tired of my company.'

'Oh! no, no, no. Dear no.'

'Go if you want to. Hate to hold anybody against their will. Hate to. Especially you. With everybody after you.'

'It's just that I find it a bit hot – I mean, there's no air—'

'Let's find somewhere cooler then. Shall we? The woods?'

The Captain hesitated about the woods. He sensed in the woods a trap far worse than the stairs. With what he hoped was an offhand gesture he swept a hand across his moustache and opened his mouth to say something even more trivial than usual when she said:

'I know. I've got the nicest, coolest idea. The river. What about the river?'

'You mean swimming?'

'No, a boat. The Larkins have a boat. In fact, two. Do you row?'

Proud of this unexpected chance to reveal another side of himself, the Captain confessed that in fact he rowed rather well. But would Larkin mind?

'Oh! Lord, no. He got the boat all ready to take me himself before lunch but Ma called us in to eat. Oh! he won't mind our taking the boat.' She laughed with a beautiful deep contralto. 'He'll just be jealous of you.'

'Will he, by Jove?'

Across the meadow lying between junk-yard and river Jasmine Brown walked deep in buttercups, her half-naked breasts thrust forward like those of some stately figurehead, her bare feet bright yellow with pollen. Once she started running and the rear view of her, its curves firmly marked and yet quivering, was of so sensational a substance that the Captain actually halted in his stride. It was only when she suddenly stopped, turned and held out both arms to him as if he were the only person in the world that he was prompted to move again.

'Come on! Race you, Colonel, race you!'

In puffing pursuit, the Captain caught her up at the boat-house, where Pop's new golden row-boat lay side by side with its sister status symbol, the motor-boat, both resplendent with purple and yellow cushions.

Stripping off his jacket, the Captain told himself that this was really where he came in. He could really show some prowess now. With a strong arm he held the boat steady while Jasmine Brown climbed in. Her body, if sensational on the stairs, was now positively volcanic in its unsparing beauty as she lay full length, every curve and contour tautly revealed, on the brilliant cushions.

The Captain got into the boat too and rowed out into a stream just wide enough at that point to take his oars. The surface of the river, broken here and there by small islands of water lilies just coming into flower, was some-times rippled by the gentlest breath of air. Now and then a leaf of yellow flag-iris twisted on the banks. A swallow or two occasionally came low over the stream, piercing the air with voices of needling excitement, but these, except for the level slip of the oars, were the only sounds.

By Jove, this, the Captain let it be known, was rather good.

'Absolute heaven.' Jasmine Brown, cool but radiating that same sensational heat of which Pop had taken such good notice, stared up at him with eyes that seemed to fill with a deep entrancement of wonder. 'You row beautifully.'

The Captain was sure that he did.

'After all I used to stroke—'

'Stroke?'

The single word seemed to be caress, flattery and invitation all in one. She raised her arms and clasped them together behind a head almost too beautiful in its frame of black hair. This gesture too seemed to be open invitation but the Captain made no sign of accepting it, and merely made steady progress with the oars. Like a cat snuggling down to half-sleep she then nestled even lower into the cushions, the soft underparts of her arms quivering, and held him with blissful, predatory, drowsy eyes.

'Come on. Do I have to drag you down here? You bring a girl out in a boat and then do absolutely nothing about it.'

The Captain, though half-terrified, could resist no longer. With nervous hands he shipped oars, stood up precariously and then half-sat, half-knelt on the cushions beside her.

The boat rocked. At the same moment Jasmine Brown seized him in an embrace as fierce and all-enfolding as that of a lioness overcoming its prey. Her splendid frame encompassed him completely. The boat rocked again and the Captain, half suffocated, uttered a stifled shout. Her lips smothered his own with a passion so well simulated that he actually found himself struggling against it and then the boat rocked a third time, this time with violence, dangerously.

A moment later the Captain, flamboyant as a tailor's dummy, flopped helplessly overboard and Jasmine Brown fell with him, shrieking with splendid laughter.

Ma's casual suggestion about telephoning the Captain's wife for tea had made Pop curiously uneasy, almost upset. He was haunted yet again by the unhappy, grovelling figure among its weeds. In moments of anything like unhappiness he always confided in Ma and now he walked round the pool to where, in her unruffled way, she was busy at her canvas under the black umbrella.

'Ma, you said summat about asking Mrs Broadbent over to tea. Why don't we? I got an idea that woman don't very often get off the hook.'

Nice idea, Ma thought. Pop had better go and get her on the blower.

'They're not on the blower. It would mean I'd have to fetch her. Think I should? It makes me miserable to—'

Certainly, Ma thought. She understood his feelings perfectly. He had so often described that moment or two of wretchedness on the path.

'Take her out of herself a bit. You go and I'll lay a

bit of quiet tea in the sitting-room. She'll very likely find it a bit noisy out here with all the kids shouting and rushing around. By the way, where's Jasmine? Haven't seen her lately.'

He hadn't the faintest, Pop said.

'Funny,' Ma said, 'that you shouldn't know after the way you've had her in your inside pocket all day.'

To this Pop could conjure no sort of answer and merely walked airily away, his habitual jauntiness back, whistling.

Some time later Mrs Broadbent, astonishingly rescued from the all-embalming boredom of Sunday afternoon, sat in the sitting-room nibbling like a mouse released from a dark box at cucumber sandwiches, chocolate biscuits and Ma's delightful maids-of-honour. An infinite shyness kept her silent for the greater part of the time. Now and then Pop, in his customary way, made springy, jovial attempts to enliven the proceedings but he noticed that she never laughed at all.

Her shy nibblings reminded him greatly of the two little Barnwell sisters, Effie and Edna, who also sometimes came to tea, their little elderly yellow faces so crowded with freckles that they looked perpetually as if stung by bees. But in their case hunger, so richly satisfied as it always was in the Larkin household, made them chatter brightly and even inspired in them, at times, fits of immoderate giggles. It was the same with Edith Pilchester; food and drink went rapidly to her head, making her tipsy with happiness and even, as Pop had often noted, a little bit sexy. He expected it was really some urge in all of them, as he frequently told Ma, that hadn't yet been satisfied.

But in Mrs Broadbent, he was sure, there was neither sex nor laughter; he doubted even if there was life apart from the mere mechanics of movement; and he was just about to reach the point of half-wishing that he'd let well alone and hadn't invited the poor woman over at all when Ma, looking out of the window, suddenly leapt up and very nearly dropped her tea-cup on the floor.

'Good Gawd Almighty,' she said, 'whatever in the name of Beelzebub has happened to the Colonel?'

Pop got casually to his feet with an air of indifferent surprise, as if the incident were, to him, totally unexpected.

'Got caught in a thunderstorm or somethink.'

The erstwhile flamboyant figure of the Captain, now dragging itself across the yard, looked like that of a ship-wrecked mariner washed up on some blighted shore.

Mrs Broadbent got slowly to her feet too and stared out of the window. She stared for perhaps some fifteen seconds or so before the room was filled with the strangest of sounds, her loud uncontrolled cascades of laughter. It was as if she had been rocked to near-hysteria by an explosion of sudden joy.

Fearful of some explosion in himself, Pop slid out of the room, to be met at the front door by Angela Snow who slipped her cool aristocratic hand in one of his.

'We didn't fail you?'

'Think everythink went perfick.'

'Good. Absolutely splendid. Well, that's one christening over, dear man. And without benefit of clergy.'

Pop laughed, kissing her with mischievous lightness on one ear, in silent thanks.

'By the way, Jasmine and I tossed up for it.'

'Did?'

'Yes: I won. But I put her in first. Hadn't you better go and find her?'

'Where do you think she is?'

'I rather fancy she's in the boat-house,' Angela Snow said, in that lovely drawling way of hers, 'waiting for a little thank-you.'

That night, sitting in bed, smoking his late cigar and watching Ma at the dressing-table, brushing her hair, Pop suddenly made a remark of casual profundity.

'Ma, I've been thinking.'

'Now steady.'

'No, serious. I mean about people, men and women.'

That was a tall one, Ma said. If he got started with that he'd be stuck with it all night. There was no end to that one.

'They're funny,' Pop said. 'People, I mean.'

Not, he hastened to assure her, people like him and Ma. Or even Angela or Jasmine. Not normal people. No, the others: some of 'em anyway. The Colonel for instance. And Mrs Broadbent.

'How do you work that one out, Ma?'

Ma said she was blessed if she knew.

'Me, neither. You'd want Solomon on that one. By the way what did you think of Jasmine?'

'Girl after my own heart.'

'Good. Thought you'd like her. Well-made, too, don't you think?'

'You should know. You were in the boat-house long enough with her before lunch today.'

'That was a sort of briefing, Ma, sort of dummy run,' Pop proceeded to explain blandly, with all his customary frankness. 'After all I'd got to get the idea into her head somehow.'

Dummy run? Ma wanted to know what on earth he was talking about. Dummy run? Idea? What idea?

'The Colonel's christening.'

Pop, laughing, started to explain about the Colonel and how Jasmine and Angela had tossed up for the privilege of performing the ceremony.

'Well, praise God from whom all blessings flow,' Ma said and burst out into one of her own uncontrollable fits of jellified laughter.

'Really, on the whole,' Pop said airily, 'I think it went orf perfick.'

Laughter, especially at night, always put Ma into the warmest and most magnanimous of moods and now she suddenly turned on him with a slow, engaging smile and said:

'You know something, Syd Larkin?'

'No, Ma. What?'

'I believe if I'd have married you,' Ma said, 'you'd have committed bigamy long ago.'

'More than likely,' Pop said with great cheerfulness, 'more than likely.'

6

On a damp dull afternoon in mid-July – it was what Ma
was accustomed to call a wet day and no rain, or alter-
natively bad courting weather – Pop drove the Rolls
Royce out of the junk-yard and, though using the
contrapuntal horn with care and frequency, almost ran
into the figure of his old friend the Brigadier, walking
dreamily in the mizzle on the road outside. The open
black umbrella he was carrying over his shoulder might
well have been borrowed from a scarecrow. One of his
shoelaces, a brown one as opposed to its fellow, which
was black, was undone and flapping muddily about its
canvas shoe. His once cream trousers hung sack-like
about his spindly legs, the behind showing a patch of
some thicker material that might possibly have come
from a bed quilt. It had a distinctly raised pattern of
flowers on it and, though once white, was now worn
to a sort of pied grey. But the Brigadier's crowning
sartorial features were new to Pop and made even him
start with surprise. The first was a pale pink rowing
blazer, of a sort of crushed raspberry shade, with a
white and black silk badge on the pocket, and the second
a small and very ancient rowing cap in a rather deeper
shade.

'What cheer, General!' Pop said, laughing with most

friendly robustness, 'must look where you're going, else we'll be having cold mincemeat for supper.'

Pop's choice of cold mincemeat as opposed to hot struck the Brigadier as a singularly apt one, if rather macabre, and woke on his face the driest of smiles. He readily confessed he'd been day-dreaming and Pop said:

'Well, hop in, General. It's no day for walking.'

The Brigadier coughed abruptly and thanked Larkin all the same but said he really preferred the exercise. It helped him, among other things, to let off steam.

'About what? Summat bothering you?'

'It's that damned common market all the time. I frequently feel my blood boil.'

'Don't like it much, eh?'

'I call it a damned unholy alliance. Damned unholy, I tell you. Always loathed the French anyway.'

In reply Pop barked out a loud and cordial "Ear 'ear!', the immediate result of which was that the Brigadier snapped down the umbrella, opened the Rolls' monogrammed front door and got inside the car.

'Changed my mind after all.' He struck Pop a sharp genial blow on the knee. 'Man after my own heart, Larkin. Man after my own heart. Where are you bound?'

Down to the coast, Pop told him. He'd got to see a man about a little deal in cats' meat. And while he was there he'd got to get Ma a pint of whelks and winkles. Did the General care for whelks or winkles?

'Not awfully, I'm afraid.'

'Ma adores 'em. Well, anyway, come for the ride. I was thinking of picking up Edith and giving her a spin. Just for company. I get the pip without company.'

'Ah! the Pilch, eh? Haven't seen her for a long time.'

Pop laughed with great vigour, at the same time letting in the clutch, so that the Rolls moved smoothly away. It always made him laugh when the General, in his drier moods, called Edith Pilchester the Pilch, though he could never tell him why. He would have to get Ma to explain to him what a pilch was one day. He didn't suppose the General knew.

'Doesn't she know you're calling? She'll probably be spinning wool or something. Or deeply engaged in making mead.'

Pop, laughing again, said if he knew Edith she'd come even if she'd broken both legs.

'The last time I saw her she was in a state of some excitement about a yellow flower she was growing,' the Brigadier said. 'Going to make woad with it, she fancied. That blue stuff, you remember, that the Ancient Britons painted their bodies with.'

'Good Gawd.'

A fantastic vision of Edith Pilchester, unclothed and painted blue, floated before Pop's eyes, leaving him otherwise speechless. You never knew what women were going to be up to next. It bowled you flat.

'Cats' meat?' the Brigadier said suddenly. 'I wasn't aware you were in the meat trade.'

Tinned, Pop explained. Big call for it nowadays. West Indians ate most of it. It was cheaper than the butcher's.

'Good grief,' the Brigadier said, feeling very faintly sick. 'What will one hear of next?'

Five minutes later Pop was poking his head round the back door of Edith Pilchester's low-pitched thatched cottage, Bonny Banks, even more gimcrack in its pseudo antiquity than Lady Violet's bungalow, and calling was anybody at home? Something like an alarmed sigh instantly answered him from one of the tiny bedroom windows, from which the head of Edith Pilchester popped out like a jack-in-the-box a moment later, her shoulders hastily covered with a shawl of her own knitting and dyeing. This was of rather an indeterminate toad-like hue and once again Pop was for a moment or two utterly silenced by the thought of what Edith might possibly look like if dipped blue all over.

'Oh! my goodness, Mr Larkin, you caught me unawares! My dear!—'

'Thought you might like to come for a trip in the Rolls. Going as far as the sea.'

'Oh! but – my dear, I'm simply not ready – it's absolutely ghastly—'

'No hurry, Edith. I can wait. I got the General with me. I'll go and talk to him.'

'Oh! will you? I'll just slip something on – I'll be down the *instant* I'm ready.' Miss Pilchester disappeared swiftly from the window, only to come back a moment later to ask with piping fervour: '*Will* I need an umbrella? *Will* I, do you think?'

'No,' Pop said, with that bland innocence of his that

79

might have concealed anything, winking at the same time. 'I'll keep you dry.'

'Awful man.' A sort of indrawn giggle fell from her lips and Pop found himself momentarily transfixed with a toothy, dedicated smile. 'You *do* put meanings into—'

An interval of a bare five or six minutes was enough to bring Edith Pilchester stumbling from the cottage in partly dishevelled haste. The slight mizzling rain had ceased by now and a burst of light wind seemed to catch her half way down the garden path and fairly blow her into the Rolls, the front door of which the Brigadier was holding open for her with a combination of his best military and rowing *politesse*. He actually raised the rowing cap as she half-crawled, half-fell into the car, giving her at the same time a dry, charming smile and saying cryptically:

'Dear lady. I trust I see you well?'

In tones of loud and hearty excitement Miss Pilchester, who had forgotten to close the door, confessed that she literally didn't know. It was all such a *thrill*, so absolutely *unexpected*. Had she been an *age*? If only she'd been able to collect her thoughts a little better, she thought wildly, she might even have been a teeny bit longer, so that perhaps Pop might have been forced to search for her, and then – Well, it was terrifically nice of him to come anyway.

'I'll just shut the door, Edith. Otherwise we'll be having you in the cold mincemeat lark too.'

'Extraordinary thought!'

80

Pop, leaning across her and lightly brushing against the cabbage-green suit of hairy sack-like material she was wearing, closed the quiet, heavy door of the Rolls. This sudden physical contact with him at a moment so early and unprepared sent a half-rapturous quiver through her body, to be followed a second or two later by an almost cataclysmic palpitation as Pop deftly and with an accuracy born of long practice pressed one of her right suspender buttons. Heaven, she would dream of this, she knew, for days.

'All right, General? Don't mind sitting at the back? Have a doss-down if you feel like it.'

'Wouldn't dream of it. Feel as lively as a cricket.'

'Perfick. We'll get crackin' then.'

As the Rolls moved regally and smoothly away Edith Pilchester felt lively as a cricket too. Another five minutes and she'd have been off to the post-office and she'd have missed it all. The thought was too absolutely ghastly.

On the luxurious dove-grey seat at the back the Brigadier started to say something and then realised that, hermetically sealed off as he was by the car's glass division, his voice couldn't be heard with anything like precision in the front. At this instant Pop barked down the speaking tube:

'Use the tube, General, old man. Use the tube.'

Hanging on to a yellow silk cord with one hand and taking up the speaking tube with the other the Brigadier gave several dry, gruff coughs and then said:

'Larkin, my dear fellow, it was in my mind to ask you something.'

'Subscription or summat?'

'No. Merely that rumour has it that some character or other nearly got drowned at your place the other day.'

'Oh! that.' Pop laughed with crackling delight into the tube. 'Just a bit o' sport, that's all.'

'Not serious then?'

'Well it was for *him*. The rest of us had a good giggle out of it.'

'It was that ghastly man, Broadbent,' Miss Pilchester said, with loud, sudden and positively tigerish ferocity. 'Damn him. I sometimes feel like braining him myself. The brute terrorises that little wife of his so that she's forgotten what talking is. He's made her into a crazy mute. He doesn't need drowning. It's too good for him. He needs the fiery furnace. Slowly, the snob.'

The unexpected savagery of this outburst had Pop temporarily speechless. With his mouth wide open he simply couldn't think of a word to say. A rapid glance at Edith revealed that in indignation she had gone a remarkable bluish shade, so that for a moment Pop was half convinced she had been dipping herself in that Ancient Briton stuff, woad or whatever it was. He'd never heard a burst from Edith like it. It was what Ma would have called real primitive.

'Do I hear Edith sitting in judgement on somebody?'

'You do, an' all, General. Shook me to the nellies.'

'Indeed?' The Brigadier was about to express himself as unfamiliar with this particular expression when Edith, in a fresh but by no means as ferocious a burst, declared ah! but they didn't know her. There was a real positive demon inside her that was terrible, absolutely ghastly and terrible, when it got roused.

'Now and then I can't help it. It just pops out.'

'Good Gawd,' Pop said and heard the Brigadier, from the luxury of the back seat, echo the words as if in a soft amen.

'Moreover, he threatens to sue you.'

'Me?' Pop said, his customary laughing self again. 'Nothing to do wiv me. He just went on the river with a piece of crumpet.'

'A piece of what?' the Brigadier said.

'Crumpet. There she is,' Pop said, 'that's her,' and having taken a picture of Jasmine Brown from his inside pocket pushed back the glass division and handed it to the Brigadier.

In stupefied silence the Brigadier gazed for several minutes at the sensational lines of Jasmine Brown reclining in a white bikini against a dark rock by the sea. It was almost too much for his elderly frame to bear and he was momentarily sad in heart when Pop unthinkingly declared down the speaking tube:

'Friend of Angela's. Job to know which is more perfick, eh?'

In silence the Brigadier handed the picture back to Pop, who in turn handed it to Edith, who also had nothing to say. Something told her that it wasn't for nothing that Pop carried this gripping picture of all-but-naked flesh about with him and it actually seemed for a moment as if the demon in her snorted its indignation at her folly and Pop's own particular brand of faithlessness but at that strategic moment Pop elected to run a caressive hand across her middle thigh, so that her tremulous veins ran with forgiving and ecstatic light again.

Two minutes later Pop was bringing the Rolls to an unexpected halt outside a small wayside white-washed pub called *The Lamb and Flag*. In the grass paddock behind the pub, between rows of dark elms, a little roundabout, a coconut shy, a pair of swings, a dart stall and a shooting gallery lit up with yellow, scarlet, green and blue the damp, dull July afternoon.

'Strike me if I don't think it's my old pal Fruity,' Pop said. 'Old Fruity Pears.'

'How's the swings and roundabouts? How's the fair lark, Fruity?'

'If it ain't me ole china Syd. If it ain't me ole china.'

The fragile monkey-faced figure in charge of the coconut shy, dressed in black trousers, a cream polo-necked sweater and a small old-fashioned black bowler, needed only a towel slung over his shoulder to be a second out of some fairground boxing ring. His toothless mouth shot open like a trap. His eyes, completely colourless, watered suddenly with surprise, disbelief and pleasure. His scrawny yellow fingers gripped Pop's hand like eager talons.

'Must be ten year. Must be ten year.'

His voice was cracked. Pop, pump-handling with friendly vigour, asked again how the fair lark was, the swings and roundabouts and all that and then, taking a swift look about him, knew there wasn't much need for an answer. Four children on the roundabout, where the fat little figure of Mrs Fruity was turning the handle, and two youths with heavy side-burns and stiff crew cuts, in black sweaters, drain-pipe jeans and winkle-pickers, made up the entire custom of the afternoon. There wasn't even any music coming from the round-about, which went round and round in silent procession, cockerels following little racing cars, peacocks after buses, like a ghostly quaking wheel.

'Finished. Busted. Thinking of turning it in. Can't compete with telly. Some days we don't take half a quid.'

Another little bit of old England gone, Pop thought, and in an immense effort to be cheerful slapped the fragile Fruity on the back, a blow which made him quiver like a straw in the wind, and then introduced his friends Miss Pilchester and the Brigadier.

Fruity, gazing at the pinkly arrayed figure of the Brigadier, said something like 'Strewth!' under his breath and silently wondered if he hadn't better start up a freak tent again, with two-headed dogs and a bearded lady, like the one he'd had twenty years ago. He'd never seen anybody quite like the Brigadier before.

'Well, we'll have to see if we can't boost the till up a bit, shan't we? What'll it be, General? Roundabouts, coconuts, swings or what? Don't have no music on the roundabout, Fruity. How's that?'

'The old organ's busted and I can't git it mended. Couldn't afford it even if I could.'

'Edith, what about you? Try the lot? Go on the swings with me? What'll you start with?'

'I should absolutely adore to knock a coconut.'

'Coconuts it is an' all then. Give us five bobs' worth o' balls, Fruity old man.'

Over at the swings the two youths in winkle-pickers were larking with the boats, swinging them at crazy angles. One boat splintered against an upright and Fruity paused at the business of handing out coconut balls to yell creakily for them to stop it and merely got a gesture of two stiff obscene fingers in reply.

'They was 'ere one day afore,' Fruity said. 'It was them what busted the old organ up. Didn't like the tunes it played. Not new enough, they said.'

'Ignore 'em,' Pop said. 'Only thing to do. Edith, your first throw.'

'The old organ cost me fifty quid when I bought it. Hi! cut that out, you young bastards! I tell you stop it, the pair of you!'

Laughing, the winkle-pickers crashed the boats again.

'Throw, Edith. Ignore 'em. Take no notice.'

With surprising force and inaccuracy Miss Pilchester hurled wooden balls at the coconuts. The Brigadier started throwing too, with no success at all and so vigorously at one attempt that his pink cap dropped off. Fruity picked it up for him, and staring at it with greater disbelief than ever, laid it on the crate of balls.

Pop also started throwing, with a mixture of athletic flourish and abandon, twice striking a coconut with such force that Edith Pilchester shrieked 'Splendid!' at top voice. Playfully, when the coconut didn't fall, Pop accused Fruity of having 'em stuck on with glue or summat and Fruity looked pained, more monkey-like than ever, and said he never went in for that sort of thing and Pop ought to know him better.

The balls were expended rapidly and Edith Pilchester cried with a sort of rapturous lack of hope that it was absolutely ghastly and that she'd never get one and it was the one thing she absolutely must have.

Pop started to call for another five bobs' worth of balls but his voice was smothered by a shattering crack of wood against wood from the direction of the swings as a boat, upended, twisted from its hooks and fell.

The alarm sent three children scurrying from the roundabouts. Fruity, his monkey face grey with rage, started running too. Pop held him back. The Brigadier thought it prudent to pick up his umbrella and started to say something about 'Hadn't they better close ranks?' when the two winkle-pickers, suddenly tired of the swing-boats as of a broken toy, started sidling across the paddock.

'Keep throwing, Edith. Ignore 'em. You'll get one yet.'

Something in Edith Pilchester's normally rather loose and ungainly frame seemed to tighten up. She limbered herself to throw and did so with such accuracy that she actually struck a coconut fair and square. For a few seconds it wobbled but failed to fall and she cried out again in typical anguish that it was absolutely ghastly.

The winkle-pickers were now at the shooting gallery. The taller of the two, who sported a thin red boot-lace tie, picked up a rifle and started loading it. Fruity yelled again and over at the roundabout Mrs Fruity hustled the remaining children away.

'Put that bloody gun down! Put it down and git orf, I tell you. Put the bloody thing down!'

The winkle-picker with red boot-lace turned and with arrogant calm pointed the gun straight at Fruity. The horror of seeing a loaded gun pointed at someone so outraged every military instinct left alive in the Brigadier that he ripped out sternly, shaking his umbrella:

'By God, don't be a damn fool! Never point a gun, you idiot!'

The tallest winkle-picker slung the gun over his shoulder, holding it by the barrel. Together the two of them sidled over to the coconuts.

'Everybody's got big mouths round here. What's all the shouting for? Everybody shouts.'

Pop turned his back and threw two balls with calm and accuracy at the coconuts.

'Keep throwing, Edith. We'll get one yet.'

'So the lady wants a coconut, does she?'

The Brigadier was pale. He thought the situation sticky. It mightn't be so bad for himself and Pop but he feared for Edith and said:

'Now look here, you fellows—'

'Belt up, Tweedledum.'

'Now, one moment—'

'So the lady wants a coconut, does she? So the lady shall have a coconut. Give the lady a coconut.'

Nobody moved.

'I said give the lady a coconut, grandad. You 'eard.'

Again nobody moved and again something seemed to tighten up in Edith Pilchester.

'All right, if grandad won't give the lady a coconut somebody else'll 'ave to.' In two lazy strides the taller winkle-picker was over by the pile of coconuts. He picked one up. He spun it in the air, turned and thrust it into Edith Pilchester's hands. 'In fact two coconuts. The lady shall 'ave two coconuts.'

He picked up another, put that into Edith Pilchester's hands too and said:

'Everybody 'appy now? We want everybody to be 'appy. Everybody 'appy? No, grandad don't look very 'appy. Why you not 'appy, grandad?'

'You leave my bloody gear alone!'

'Nobody's not touching no gear. Nobody's not touching nothing. Not touching nothing, are we, Jed?'

Jed said no, nobody wasn't touching nothing.

'I ought to bust your clock in!' Fruity said, 'you ignorant bastard.'

'You called me that once already, grandad, but not no more.'

The butt of the rifle made a short swinging stab through the air. It struck the left side of Fruity's monkey face just behind the ear. Without a cry he made an almost trance-like fall over the pile of coconuts, pouring blood.

Pop, not often enraged, turned with fury, only to find the shorter of the two winkle-pickers, Jed, pointing an open razor straight at the pit of his stomach.

'Go on, stick it in. I'll just bleed shandy.'

'No funny business. Back over there. Go on, back.'

The razor made sinister bright passes at the air and Pop backed seven or eight paces away from the coconut shy. Nobody said a word and the dull damp afternoon seemed curiously dead until suddenly a cataclysmic fury broke out in the form of the demon rising out of Edith Pilchester.

With an accuracy born of pure rage she hurled a coconut. It struck the shorter winkle-picker dead in the small of the back. His surprise was not merely infinite. It paralysed him where he stood. His fingers stiffened open with shock and he dropped the razor.

Pop, stooping to pick it up, was confronted by the extraordinary spectacle of Edith Pilchester running amok or going berserk or whatever it was they called it. He'd never seen anything like it. The demon was in full cry. A second coconut struck the shorter winkle-picker in precisely the same place as the first. The thud of it sickened the air and he crumpled slowly to his knees with a sort of gulping tender sigh.

A moment later Edith Pilchester started madly hurling coconut balls in all directions. Pop, having now picked up the razor and turning just in time to see the red-tie winkle-picker in sharp retreat, found himself in a shower of wooden rain. Balls were falling wildly all about him and one, straight as an arrow, hit him full in the left eye, as plumb as could be.

Half-blind but undaunted he tore after the retreating winkle-picker. He caught him by the top scruff of his crew cut with one hand and with the nimblest of gestures slit the razor through the thin leather belt with the other. The slow resulting fall of the trousers half way to his knees brought from Edith Pilchester a low howl, which in turn rose to a scream and finally to a great burst of demonaic laughter.

The Brigadier, helping Mrs Fruity to staunch Fruity's blood with a handkerchief, paused to utter cryptic congratulations.

'Well played, Edith, good show. Stout fellow, Larkin.'

Edith, coming out of a sort of mad trance, could only stare at Pop's face and howl again. My dear, how in heaven's name had she come to do anything so absolutely ghastly? Pop, in turn, felt momentarily a bit cock-eyed and started to walk round in odd circles. The eye was going to be a beauty.

It was enough to make you die laughing, though, in a way, he thought. He'd never seen anything like it. It was almost worth a shiner to see Edith like that. It really made you wonder what was inside people and suddenly he actually began laughing and said:

'Well, we've had the winkle-pickers but somehow I don't think Ma'll get her whelks and winkles now. We'd better get old Fruity to a doctor.'

Back at home, Ma looked with remarkably dispassionate interest at the eye, now darkening beautifully, and asked what had happened to the other fellow?

'It was a woman.'

'Oh? Well, I'm always telling you how you'll end up.'

Pop proceeded to explain, with an almost light brevity, that it had, in fact, been Edith.

'Oh? Went too far for once?'

'No. Nothing like that. She hit me with a coconut ball.'

At this Ma laughed so much that she couldn't get her breath for several minutes and had to be thumped hard on the back by Pop, just as if she'd swallowed a fish-bone. For a time Pop seriously thought she was going to have one of her turns.

When she had calmed herself again and dried her eyes Pop apologised about the whelks and winkles but said that after all he and Edith and the Brigadier had really been very busy with other things. Ma said it didn't matter a bit: she'd make do with a drop of champagne and smoked salmon instead.

Coming home the following evening from visiting Fruity in hospital, where he had taken him a few modest comforts such as grapes, strawberries, cherries, half a pound of tobacco, a bottle of whisky and a tin of butter-balls, Pop kissed Ma in prolonged and passionate greeting, as if he hadn't seen her for a month or so, and then said, laughing, that he had a big surprise for her. Could she guess what?

'How many guesses?'

'Three.'

'Well, I'll start with women.'

Rather to Ma's surprise – though she never really experienced any very deep or protracted surprise at anything Pop said or did – Pop said no, it wasn't wimmin.

'Funny. By the way your eye's come up lovely.'
There was something peculiarly funny about the eye;
she very nearly collapsed every time she looked at it.
'Hurt much? Shall I put a bit more steak on it?'

No, it was a waste of good steak, Pop thought. Next
guess?

'Not been drowning anybody again?'

Pop said no and what was more he'd never drowned
anybody anyway.

'Charley says it was a good job too. He says it's
what's called being an accessory before the fact.'

'Never? Accessory, what's that? Blimey. One more
guess.'

Ma, laughing warmly, said she hoped it hadn't got
anything to do with any more Regency pots? and Pop
said no, it wasn't that either.

'Well, go on then. You'd better make a clean breast
of it straight away.'

Pop, who by this time had lit up one of his Havanas,
blew exquisite smoke, looking exceptionally pleased
with himself. He looked what Ma called extra cocka-
tooish, almost like he sometimes did just before he got
half-whistled, so that she could only guess he must have
brought off some very nice deal.

'No, as a matter of fact, Ma,' he said, 'I just bought a
fair.'

'Oh! really? A fair? What sort? Roundabouts and
that?'

'Swings, coconut shy, shooting gallery, one roundabout and a dart stall.'

'Oh! really?' Ma said. 'Sounds very nice. Where'd you pick that up?'

Pop went on to explain about Fruity: how the telly and all that had pretty nigh ruined Fruity and how, what with one thing and another, getting old and teddy boys playing him up and now the blow on the conk, he felt he couldn't carry on. Had to sell out.

'Felt I had to make it up to him somehow. Might never have happened if me and Edith and the General hadn't been there. After all it practically all started with Edith and her coconuts. By the way the doctor says if Fruity hadn't been wearing his bowler he'd have been in Kingdom Come.'

'Makes you sick.'

'Edith's looking a bit pale round the gills an' all too today. Says she can't understand it. Can't think what got into her. I told her it was the Ancient Briton coming out in her.'

Oh? Ma said, unperturbed by this inconsequential reference to the distant Britannic past, how did he account for that then?

'Sort of throw-back,' Pop said. 'She's been making woad or something. The General told me.'

Woad? Ma said. Something to drink, wasn't it?

'No, that's mead,' Pop said. 'This woad stuff was what the Ancient Britains painted their bodies with. She's going to dye wool with it. Blue, it is.'

Really, Ma said. Still, they did funny things in those days, though she supposed it wasn't all that different, when you came to think of it, from rubbing yourself with sun-tan lotion and all that.

'Suppose not,' Pop said.

'By the way, who do you think you're going to sell this fair to?'

Pop, looking mildly pained at this question, said:

'Sell it, Ma? Sell it?'

'Course. Got to hock it to somebody, haven't you?'

'Not going to hock it, Ma. No fear. Going to keep it. For myself. For the kids. For us.'

'Us? Bit on the big side, don't you think?'

Pop's voice immediately took on that special tone of velvet fervour he reserved for more eloquent soliloquies on his beloved countryside, its nightingales and black-birds, bluebells and primroses, hay-time and high summer; and above all his beloved England.

It was, he went on to explain to Ma, – the fair, he was talking about – a little bit of old England. He wanted to save it for himself. Very like, in a few years, you wouldn't see no more fairs, like Fruity's, in little paddocks, behind little pubs. They would all be gone, like harvest home and may-poles and all that. The telly would have killed 'em all like it killed everything. Pop was getting tired of telly. They were all going boss-eyed, watching telly. What was on tonight anyway?

Ma said she thought there was nothing on worth watching at all. It was all a load of rubbish, like old Monty talking about winning the battle of Agincourt.

'Got the wrong battle, haven't you, Ma?' After all they'd got to be fair to old Monty. They'd named a son after him.

'Well, they're all the same,' Ma said. 'Battles. Not

a pin to choose between 'em. They make you tired.'

'Going back to the fair,' Pop said. 'It might sound sentimental and all that to some folks. But that's how it is. That's how I feel.'

'Where are you going to put it anyway?'

In the paddock, he told her. He was going to have the old busted organ repaired too, so that they could have a bit of gay music. He'd already asked Fruity what sort of tunes the old thing played and Fruity remembered there was *Waiting For the Robert E. Lee, Lily of Laguna* and several others, including that waltz, *Gold and Silver.* Did Ma remember that waltz? They'd danced to it a good few times in the old days.

'And I'll tell you what else I thought.'

'Yes?' Ma said. 'What was that?'

'I thought we'd open it for the christening. I thought it would be just the job for the christening.'

Nicest idea he'd had yet, Ma said. Like Mariette often said, he really did have the nicest ideas sometimes. The fair would make it a real good day. Oh! and that reminded her of something. Was he aware that the christening was only ten days away and what had he done, if anything, about thinking up a nice present each for the two god-mothers? Of course she hadn't much experience of christenings but she thought it would be nice. She thought it was probably the done thing.

'Present? Such as what?'

'Something personal, I should think. Nice set of under-clothes. Nice nightie. A nice nightie's never in the way.'

Pop started to roar with laughter and Ma said:

'Never mind. You know what I mean. And there's another thing. Don't forget you've got to go and meet Mademoiselle Dupont off the boat.'

Pop said he hadn't forgotten; he had, in fact, given a lot of thought to that.

'Serious, I hope?' Ma said. 'She's come a long way and we want to make a good impression. After all it's her first visit to England and we don't want her to go away with any wrong ideas. Even if she is French.'

Pop cordially agreed. They most certainly didn't. They had to make a good impression and, as he got up to stroll in the garden and finish his cigar and listen for a few moments to a late nightingale pouring song on the cool summer air, assured Ma that they most certainly would.

'After all, Froggies are human, I suppose, Ma. In a way.'

7

Mademoiselle Dupont stood in the sunshine on the deck
of the cross-channel steamer and gazed at the cream-
white cliffs of Dover, crowned by their gigantic grey
brooding lion of a castle, with a mixture of strange and
conflicting emotions. Normally a person of a temperament tautly if not highly strung, she had experienced
all day an apprehension verging on fear, a happiness at
times very near to sickness and a sense of wondering
expectancy so irrational that several times she had
desperately wished she could turn and go back to France
again. After all it wasn't every day that you went to stay
in the house of an English milord.

Deeply binding these feelings into a strong physical
tension was a sense of almost primitive suspicion. Not a
suspicion of anything or anybody in particular: merely a
deep-rooted, peasant-blooded suspicion of being abroad,
in a strange new country. For this reason she had put all
her money into a suède leather belt which she had
buckled under her corsets, had taken half a dozen aspirins
against the dreaded likelihood of *mal de mer* and the
paralysing excitements of travelling in general and had
put on two sets of underclothes and two thick woollen
jumpers against England's notorious, crippling, even
killing dampness. A deep superstition that she would be

inevitably accosted by strange men or have her pocket picked had also made her put on dark glasses; by some illogical process of thought she felt she wouldn't be seen so easily that way. The result of all this was that her stomach, even though the sea was soft and calm, seemed to have risen to the level of her too tightly corseted bust and was full of an astringent, contracting bile.

These insurances against fate and the half-dread of England's shores were, however, small against the greater precaution she had taken with luggage. Five suitcases and a giant blue-and-green plaid hold-all contained among other things twenty dresses, six jumpers, eight nightdresses, a great assortment of lingerie and stockings, several pairs of heavy woollen bed socks, several scarves, three overcoats, two mackintoshes, seven hats and four bottles of cough cure.

It was her unshakable conviction that the social and domestic life in the house of an English milord would inevitably take her in a bewildering, paralysing grip. Every eventuality, from cocktail parties to dinners, tennis parties to race-meetings, tea parties to gymkhanas, not to speak of the christening itself, had had to be covered. And she had, she thought, covered them all.

After the boat had docked she found herself a porter, who wanted to know if she would be travelling by car or by train.

'By car,' she told him. 'And it will be a Rolls Royce.'

'Very good, lady. Meet you outside the station.'

The porter's words merely served as yet another cause

for misgiving. She suddenly experienced the fear that Milord Larkin wouldn't be there to meet her. Something would have gone wrong. She would find herself deserted, her day in ruins.

Things were even worse when a customs officer took a not unsuspicious view of a Frenchwoman with five large suitcases and an even larger hold-all and it was nearly half an hour before she found herself outside the station, hot and flustered in her overweight woollens, looking for the Rolls.

To her intensely emotional relief it was there. She nearly wept. Pop too was there and with him someone who, dressed as he was in a pink jacket and small pink peaked cap, she could only think was some kind of old retainer, a footman or something of that sort.

'*Ah! bon jour, Mademoiselle!*' Pop, advancing cheerily into waves of lily-of-the-valley perfume, kissed her with gallantry on both cheeks, having been strictly warned by Ma not to kiss her on the lips in public, as this would undoubtedly upset her. Kissing on the lips in public wasn't, she understood, quite the thing in France. Nor was he to call her froggy. '*Comment allez-vous?* Had a good journey? Nice crossing?'

'*Merveilleux, Monsieur Larkin,*' she said, pronouncing Larkin in the French way and oh! how good it was to see him.

'This is the General,' Pop said, with another show of gallantry. 'And, General, this is Mademoiselle Dupont.'

The Brigadier, bowing with a certain military stiffness, expressed himself as delighted to meet her and held open the back door of the Rolls. The shining monograms seemed positively to wink in the sun. And odd though the elderly retainer's uniform was – she almost supposed it was some medieval survival or something of that sort – Mademoiselle Dupont nevertheless felt a wave of flattery that completely calmed the last of her fears until she suddenly remembered something.

'*Quelle horreur, mes bagages!* Where is my baggage?'

'All is well, dear lady,' the Brigadier said. 'All in the boot. All taken care of.'

With a final gulp of relief she sat back on the Rolls luxurious cushions and the Brigadier, with a certain air of old-world circumspection, closed the door.

Pop decided that this was a good moment to have a mint humbug. Ma didn't like smoking in the Rolls; it made it smell like a four-ale bar. Nevertheless Pop often felt he had to have something to chew on while driving and mint-humbugs were the answer.

'Mint humbug, General?'

The Brigadier courteously declined the offer of a mint-humbug, at which Pop said:

'Perhaps Mademoiselle Dupont would like one. Mind asking her?'

The mint-humbugs were large, rather like big gold-striped snails, and sticky. Mademoiselle Dupont, when offered one by the elderly pink-uniformed retainer, could only think it strange. Perhaps it was some old English custom which it would have been discourteous to refuse?

When she had put the mint-humbug into her mouth, where it clashed with some awkwardness against the top plate of her false teeth, the Brigadier got into the front seat of the Rolls with Pop, who now made instant use of the speaking tube.

'Well, Mademoiselle Dupont, this is England!' he called to her, as if this astonishing truth were in danger of being overlooked or something.

Mademoiselle Dupont, now completely tongue-tied by the mint-humbug, could only utter some unintelligible mumble in reply.

'Well, sit yourself back and make yourself comfortable now,' Pop called. 'We'll be home in half an hour.'

Ma, supremely anxious to make the best of impressions, had placed dark red and bright yellow roses in the silver flower vases at the back of the Rolls and these, rich and beautifully scented, gave an air of great aristocracy to the interior, almost a sense of royalty.

England, here urban, there pastoral, here downland, there a forest of television aerials, glided in its odd and entrancing mixture of scenes and styles past the windows of the Rolls. Every bit as anxious as Ma was to make the best of impressions, Pop now and then threw casual and concise information into the speaking-tube.

'See that hill? Used to be called Caesar's camp. Now turns out it was probably your bloke, William the Conqueror. Very old church just coming up. And a pub. Very old as well. *The Saracen's Head*. Something to do with the wars of the Roses.'

'The Holy Wars,' the Brigadier reminded him. 'The Crusades.'

Pop said he was very sorry. His mistake. Holy wars.

Crusades. Very old anyway. He was supremely anxious to stress the fact that everything was very old and now inquired if Mademoiselle Dupont was familiar with the word pub? Pubs were a great feature of the land; Pop didn't know what they'd do without 'em.

Mademoiselle Dupont, rather despondently engaged in unequal struggle with the mint-humbug, which among other things was now making her perspire stickily, could only slobber, offering no word in reply, so that Pop confided to the Brigadier that he thought she'd gone deaf or something since he last saw her.

'More probably extreme shyness.'

'Could be. She's a bit the nervous type.'

'By no means unattractive.'

You were telling him, Pop said and promptly recalled not unpassionate moments in bedrooms at the *Hotel Beau Rivage* which Mademoiselle Dupont kept at St. Pierre le Port in Brittany, at the same time inviting the Brigadier to admire the cuff-links she had given him as a farewell present a few summers before.

'Bit in love with me. Had a job to hold her back once or twice.'

To this modest confession the Brigadier offered no comment and Pop said:

'Got her a present too. For the christening. Set of underwear. Ma thought it would be the thing. Black. Sort you can see through.'

'Not in danger of being misinterpreted?'

Pop said he didn't think so; she was old enough to know what was what by now.

Mademoiselle Dupont, who had now been able satisfactorily to disengage herself from the mint-humbug, which she had popped into her handkerchief and thence into her handbag, thought England looked remarkably pretty as she gazed from the windows of the Rolls. Oats were turning to a beautiful pinkish yellow in some fields; in others wheat bore on it a kind of bloom, almost blue, that heralded full ripening, and everywhere along the hedgerows wild roses and honeysuckle were in full, abundant bloom. She wasn't disappointed.

What she was really looking for, however, were the great houses. She had conjured up in her mind, over and over again, a picture of an English house such as that milord Larkin might live in. Rejecting the idea of moats, drawbridges, turreted walls and battlements as being perhaps almost too much to expect, she nevertheless knew it would be old, probably in that style of black-and-white timbering she had often seen in travel magazines, with tall, fine chimneys and black oak doors, and certainly full of calm, peace and dignity.

A few moments later the Rolls went past exactly such a house and all the thrill of long pent-up expectancy shot through her, actually making her cry out with emotion and excitement.

'Ah! that house! – ah! how really most beautiful!'

'Very old,' Pop assured her. 'Manor house. Very like Elizabethan.'

'Ah! manoir. La Reine Elizabeth.'

This, this was it, she thought; this was what she had come for.

'Home in about five minutes,' Pop called down the speaking-tube.

'Sounds extraordinarily excited all of a sudden,' the Brigadier said. 'Still, the Gallic temperament, I suppose. Odd how very different they are from us, especially when you think how much of their blood really runs in ours.'

'Well, foreign, ain't they?' Pop said, as if this explained, even if it didn't condone, all sins.

'By the way,' the Brigadier said, 'what time is the christening on Sunday?'

'Twelve o'clock. Midday. Afterwards you're all coming to lunch – you, Angela, Jasmine, Edith, Mademoiselle Dupont, the Rev. Candy, the lot. Going to have a marquee. Ma's going to lay it out with stacks of cold stuff. Plenty of champagne – three colours, ordinary, pink and red – and barrels o' beer and cider. And then when that lot's gone down we'll open the fair. Got the old organ fixed – plays some very nice old tunes.'

'Clearly going to be quite an event.'

'It is an' all. First time me and Ma have had a wholesale christening anyway, I'll tell you. And probably the last. Still, you never know.'

A few minutes later Pop drew up the Rolls in the Larkin yard, riotously sounding first the town horn and then the country one to announce his arrival, the continuous contrapuntal clamour disturbing geese, turkeys, hens, guinea-fowl, pigs, ponies and all the rest and finally bringing Ma, Primrose and Victoria running from the house in greeting.

In the back of the Rolls Mademoiselle Dupont passed from a temporary state of paralysis into a dark bad dream. Her vision of calm antiquity, of dignity distilled from the aristocratic wine of centuries, disappeared under a mad, ruinous mess of muck-heaps, rusty iron, old oil drums, decaying tractors, nettles, haystacks, crumbling hovels and all the rest of Pop's perfick paradise. An earthquake could hardly have shattered her more; and as she finally bestirred herself, shocked and actually trembling, and saw the old pink-coated retainer holding open the door of the Rolls for her – no, he couldn't possibly be an old retainer, after all, she thought, he could only be a member of some strange exclusive English club – she was desperately near to tears.

So much so that she hardly heard Pop's stentorian announcement of 'Well, 'ere we are!' and in confused desperation dived into her handbag for her handkerchief, which she pressed nervously to her face so that for the space of about a second the mint-humbug was stuck there.

A moment later it fell off and as if at this signal one of the twins switched on a gramophone at the open sitting-room window, where it blared out *La Marseillaise*, while the other switched on the lights in the suits of armour, so that the two vizored heads grinned out in blue, red and yellow welcome, convincing Mademoiselle Dupont that she was the centre of some awful, garish, medieval nightmare.

8

While Mademoiselle Dupont, overwhelmed by the day's too powerful emotions, retired to her room and there sobbed inconsolably into her pillow, Ma proceeded to remonstrate rather severely with Pop, particularly in the matter of the mint-humbug, actually calling him Sydney Larkin several times, which he was fully aware was the greatest expression of reprimand she could muster.

'If I thought you'd been larking about with the poor dear and upsetting her, Sydney Larkin, I wouldn't half give you what for with the chill off. I might even keep you *rationed*—'

'Good Gawd, Ma, steady. I never done a thing—'

'Well, I believe you. Thousands wouldn't. All I can say is you'll have to make it up to her. She's started off with a very bad impression and that was the last thing I wanted. You'll have to be very, very nice to her.'

'Yes, but—'

'Never mind yes, but. You go and be nice to her. Taken her present up yet? No? Well then, go and take it up. And then ask her to come down for a champagne cocktail. No Red Bulls or Moon-Rockets or that lark tonight. She wants her nerves calming. And you've got to keep sober too.'

'Good Gawd, Ma, have a bit of heart. You sound as if you'd got the pip.'

Shortly afterwards Pop proceeded to marshal all his forces of diplomatic gallantry. He found the set of lingerie, which Ma had wrapped in a box with mauve and silver paper round it and a big broad yellow ribbon, and took it upstairs. For a few moments he considered getting Primrose, whose French was pretty fair, to write some few well-chosen words of French greeting on a card, but Primrose was in the bathroom, shampooing her hair in readiness for Sunday, and he decided to give the idea the go-by.

'Mademoiselle Dupont?' With quite uncharacteristic discretion Pop tapped very gently on her bedroom door. 'Mademoiselle Dupont? May I come in?'

There was no answer.

'Mademoiselle? Have a word with you?'

Presently he heard her footsteps coming across the bedroom floor and the key turning in the lock. Then the door opened and a singularly depressed-looking Mademoiselle Dupont stood before him, eyes crimson and downcast. She had clearly been copiously weeping.

'Bear up now, bear up!' Pop said with the tenderest sort of cheerfulness. 'Mustn't turn the milk sour. Worse things happen at sea.'

Mademoiselle Dupont, who couldn't for the life of her understand what the sea had to do with her own particular distress, said nothing. Her lips merely trembled.

'*Pour vous*,' Pop said, holding out the gay silver, mauve and yellow parcel, '*avec amour*.'

'*Pas pour moi? Non?*'

'*Oui, oui.* Little present. From me. Sort of welcome to England.'

Pop, who was nowhere near as bi-lingual as Mademoiselle Dupont, now decided to give French the go-by too. It was a lot of fag really and he'd only get himself all tangled up. He was however astute enough to remember a French gesture and with something like courtliness he bent and kissed her hand. This was entirely the wrong thing to have done, as it turned out, because she instantly started weeping again, not very loudly, but with very low, heartfelt sobs.

Pop, half afraid that Ma would hear and start giving him the old salt and vinegar again, led her into the bedroom and shut the door. He had already decided that comfort had better take a physical form, with as few words as possible. With this in mind he put his arm round her waist and squeezed her several times, the pressure positive but not urgent – very far from the sort of thing that, in Ma's words, would bring her to the boil.

Eventually she sat on the bed, with the parcel on her knees, and started muttering muted words of apology and how it was all so strange. She supposed she had become ridiculously over-excited. Pop didn't say a word but merely continued with the physical treatment, which presently began to have some success, so that she actually dried her eyes and prepared to undo the parcel.

'You should not do this. I am very foolish. I do not deserve such things.'

'Well, open it anyway,' Pop said and was on the point

of adding some quip about trying it on for size when he remembered Ma's strict injunctions and merely said: 'It's from me. A present for the christening.'

By no means tranquil yet, Mademoiselle Dupont untied the yellow ribbon with fingers that now and then jumped electrically. They jumped even more when she finally had the parcel open and picked out from among white layers of tissue paper a black bra, a black slip and a pair of black briefs so scanty and transparent that they might have been made for the sole purpose of revealing more than they covered.

It was a moment of such transcendent and palpitating intimacy and altogether so utterly unexpected that she was completely speechless and went very red. It was also a moment that Pop could resist no longer, warnings from Ma or not, and he said, in the lowest and most engaging of whispers:

'Just about your size, eh?'

'Monsieur Larkin!'

In answer Pop kissed her with considerable pressure on her left ear, with the result that one of the long pearl drop earrings that she always wore to give her shortish figure the illusion of greater height fell off and slipped down the front of her dress, inside the bosom. Pop, though on the verge of executing some instantaneous rescue act, decided it was perhaps rather early days after all and instead merely invited her, in his best free and easy fashion, to stand up and shake the bag.

She stood up and shook herself several times, but without success. The tightness of her corset and the fact that she had been too *distrait* to take off her money belt stopped the earring on its journey, though not before the slide of the earring against her body had produced in her a strange, beautifully irritant sensation, so that she actually began laughing, with a real touch of merriment, and for the first time.

'No luck? Got lost on the way,' Pop said and wondered where.

She laughed again and slowly, in this way, became soothed and mollified. The nightmare of the afternoon receded. England seemed not so bad after all. Kindness and generosity were in the air.

She duly thanked Pop several times for the gift he had made and said she would try never to be so foolish again. In turn Pop led her to the bedroom window and showed her the second of the day's great surprises. There was, as it turned out, still a third to come but now, as she gazed down at the roundabout, the swings, the coconut shies, the dart stall and the big white marquee already erected in the paddock beyond the junk-yard, she actually cried out with disbelief and delight. The English were a strange, strange people. One could only think that they were, in the nicest degree, mad. They wore strange pink coats and caps. They had fairs in their back gardens and suits of armour on their doorsteps. They were beyond all understanding.

'Notice the French flag?' Pop said.

Pop had caused a second tricolor to be run up on the marquee.

'*Ah! le tricolore!*'

'For you,' Pop said. 'In honour of you.'

Then suddenly some of her mystification cleared.

'Ah! it is a sort of *pardon*. Yes?'

No, Pop told her, it wasn't a *pardon*. It was just for the christening. He'd bought the fair specially.

She again marvelled at this, with another loud 'Ah!' and Pop said:

'Might as well make a proper do of it. After all there's a lot o' people to be christened.'

This was again beyond her understanding and everything now seemed stranger still.

When they finally went downstairs it was to find that the Rev. Candy had arrived. Mr Candy, who was in a state of bewilderment as great as that of Mademoiselle Dupont, perhaps greater, had called to acquaint himself with the Sunday order of battle. He hadn't been sleeping very well. The moon had been coming to its full. Night after night, restless-eyed, his mind jumping about like a kangaroo, he had grappled with the problem of the christening. It wasn't merely that there were so many people to be christened. It wasn't merely that he was certain he would forget more than half those long fanciful strings of Larkin names. It was the awful intimate familiarity of the thing. It was the discomforting nature of the Larkin beauty. It was having to baptise a schoolgirl who was practically, in body as well as intent, a grown woman. It was that dreadful moment when he would have to touch her head with water and she would torment him with those too dark, too luscious eyes.

'Mr Candy, this is Mademoiselle Dupont. From

France. Going to be little Oscar's godmother. That's one of his names. Dupont.'

The Rev. Candy and Mademoiselle Dupont shook hands, each nervous. Mr Candy, his timidity now accentuated into further complexity by the unexpected presence of a strange Frenchwoman, then sat down at the table, where he had already spread out several sheets of blank paper. Ma was sitting at the table too and now, after sympathetically inviting Mademoiselle Dupont to take an easy chair and at the same time giving Pop an old-fashioned look or two, as if suspicious that he hadn't been behaving very well, said:

'Pop, you get the champagne while me and Mr Candy work these names out.' She laughed broadly, shaking like a jelly. 'We don't want little Oscar christened Primrose or Victoria called Blenheim if it comes to that. Sometimes I half forget what some of 'em are called myself.'

Pop laughed too and said he was blowed if he didn't too, sometimes, and went to find the champagne, asking as he went:

'Red champagne, Ma, or ordinary?'

'Oh! ordinary,' Ma said. 'We had red last night.'

The mere mention of Primrose's name brought on the Rev. Candy a further attack of the acutest apprehension. But at least it was a relief that she wasn't there. He thanked heaven, at any rate, for that blessing. Nor was Mariette and he could only pray, tonight, that he wouldn't be called upon to give an opinion of her figure as seen in all its naked wonder by Ma.

'Now Mrs Larkin, in what order would you like the christenings to be? I mean the babies first or?—'

Oh! it was all one to her, Ma said.

'Well, may I suggest we start with the babies, since the ceremony is bound to be rather protracted.'

All right, Ma said, they'd better start with Blenheim.

'And what are his full names to be?'

'John Marlborough Churchill Blenheim Charlton,' Ma said.

The Rev. Candy wrote this down with slow and dutiful care and put the figure one against it.

'And then Oscar. It is Oscar, isn't it?'

'Yes. Oscar Columbus Septimus Dupont Larkin.'

'Ah! Septimus the seventh. I must say you've shown the most extraordinary imagination in choosing your children's names.'

'Oh?' Ma said. 'It's not everybody who's got it.'

'I once knew a man named Decius. The tenth.'

'Get away with you,' Ma said. 'You'll be putting ideas into my head.'

Deep in further embarrassment the Rev. Candy wrote hard again, eventually pausing to say:

'And who next?'

Ma said she thought it ought to be the twins next. They were always as full of mischief as a pair of magpies and it'd be better to get 'em out of the way. They were fair devils sometimes. She wouldn't put anything past 'em – even in church.

Oh! Lord, Mr Candy thought. Great Heaven.

Pop now came back into the room with a tray of

champagne cocktails, all jewelled with bubbles and invitingly golden, with half moons of orange floating about in them, and proceeded to offer them to Mademoiselle Dupont, Ma and Mr Candy.

Ma took hers with a vast sigh of satisfaction, as if she hadn't had a glass of anything for a month or more and an eager 'Ah! just what I wanted' and Mademoiselle Dupont hers with a certain restrained finesse, the little finger of her right hand delicately extended. Amazement at the nature, content and doings of the Larkin house danced in her mind as quickly and effervescently as the bubbles rising in the glasses and she merely uttered a low bi-lingual phrase of thanks.

To Pop's infinite astonishment the Rev. Candy, on the other hand, refused the cocktail. Pop felt less hurt than concerned at this extraordinary behaviour and said:

'No? Sure? Not feeling dicky or anything?'

Mr Candy said No, it wasn't that he was feeling dicky or anything. It was merely – he was too shy to confess that he dreaded not being able to keep a clear head – it was simply that he wanted to be sure of getting all the names down correctly. Perhaps he might have a *soupçon* later?

Pop, who hadn't the faintest notion what a *soupçon* was, uttered a hearty 'Course, course,' and said he'd be mixing a new lot up in a minute or two.

'And the twins?' the Rev. Candy said. 'Might I now have the names of the twins?'

Ma took a deep gulp of champagne and said Oh! the twins were fairly easy. They almost had the same names.

'One's Zinnia June Florence Nightingale and the other's Petunia June Florence Nightingale.'

As he wrote down these names the Rev. Candy was struck by another awful thought. The twins were dreadfully, dangerously alike; they were like two eggs; he would never tell them apart.

'I wonder,' he said, 'will they be differently dressed? Or perhaps they have some distinguishing mark I could note? A mole or something?'

'Well,' Ma said, giving one of her deeper, fruitier chuckles, 'Zinnia's got a mole, but not where you'd be likely to see it in church.'

'Could they wear, perhaps, different dresses? Or different coloured hair ribbons?'

Ma said she thought hair ribbons. What about a scarlet one for Zinnia and a purple one for Petunia? Same colour as the flowers.

The Rev. Candy said he thought this would do and carefully wrote the colours down, at the same time saying to Ma that he profoundly hoped they wouldn't – he was going to say 'try anything on' – but hastily added the words 'make any confusion' instead.

'They'd better not,' Ma said, 'or I'll warm their bottoms. And in church too, if I have to.'

'That I fancy, is four,' the Rev. Candy said. 'Exactly how many more have we?'

'Four,' Ma said. 'We're half way.'

'Like dipping a flock o' sheep,' Pop said. 'Eh?'

It was indeed, Mr Candy thought, and could only hope and trust that the Lord would make him a good shepherd.

Ma then proceeded to give him the full names of Montgomery and Mariette and while all this was going on Mademoiselle Dupont listened in a growing trance of disbelief and wonder. Half hypnotised as she was already by the vastness of the Larkin television set, the lavish and even grotesque nature of Pop's cocktail cabinet, all glass and chromium, in the form of a galleon, she now found herself facing the even more grotesque fact that, apparently, none of the considerable concourse of Larkins had ever received the blessing of holy baptism. This incredible and shocking fact had her, as Pop might have said, on the floor. It revived in her the strong belief that there was something outlandish about England – something, well – the *mot juste* escaped her and she merely sipped champagne in silent reflection, at a loss even for a silent word.

'And who is next?' the Rev. Candy said.

'Me. I mean I'm next now but I don't want to be then. I'd like to be last. Somebody's got to be last and Victoria doesn't want to be.'

Mr Candy looked up to see that the vision he dreaded, that of Primrose, had suddenly entered the room. He quailed silently. The already too beautiful black hair, freshly shampooed and brushed, glowed deeply, with dark blue lights in it. Every separate hair seemed to vibrate; the entire mass of it was a thick and tremulous wave. It might have been washed in the juice of elderberries and anointed with oil of roses. There was a strong seductive fragrance in the air.

'Well, I suppose that's all right,' Ma said. 'Somebody's got to provide the finishing touch.'

That, the Rev. Candy thought, was what he feared and he was now dismayed to see Primrose sit down at the table, directly opposite him. He looked down hard at his papers and quailed once again at the precocious, womanly air of the girl in front of him. She was wearing a shortish mauve dressing gown, quite open at the neck, and he could have sworn that she was wearing little, if anything, underneath it. The soft, sallow skin of her neck curved away into a taut bust uplifted and enlarged by the particular way she folded her arms underneath it. She ran her tongue over her lips, moistening them slightly, and fixed him with dark, still eyes.

'You don't mind if I'm last, Mr Candy, do you?'

'Oh! no, no, no, no, no.'

'You really don't?'

'No, no. Of course not. Of course.'

'I'm so glad.'

There was no other escape from this disquieting piece of temptation, apart from running like a hare, except to ask, as Mr Candy now did, in one of his squeakier moments:

'And may I – I – please – have your names?'

'I've got one more than all the rest,' Primrose said.

Oh! Lord, Mr Candy thought, it simply wasn't fair.

'Born bang in the middle o' spring,' Pop explained. 'Drop o' champagne now, Mr Candy? Beautiful spring too, it was an' all. Rich. Busted out all of a sudden. Everythink was sort of in calf all at once.'

Something in the Rev. Candy surrendered. He confessed weakly that he would indeed like a drop of champagne. The vision of the world in calf, in all its reproductive splendour, was too much. The champagne cocktail was like liquid manna to his soul.

'And what, please, are your names?'

As Primrose said each of her names in reply the exact expression in her eyes seemed to change by an infinitesimal fraction, but Mr Candy's own eyes were downcast, so that he was mercifully saved the sight of these variations on a seductive theme.

'Primrose, Violet, Anemone, Iris, Magnolia, Narcissa.'

At the name Narcissa Mr Candy was compelled to look up; and the open face of the purest white narcissus could hardly have faced him across the table with greater innocence. He quailed yet again before the sheer candour of its charm.

'Narcissa? Or Narcissus?'

'Narcissa.'

'Prettier than the "us" at the end, don't you think?' Ma said.

'Oh! much, much.'

'I think so,' Ma said and then proceeded to put to Mr Candy a devastating theory of her own. 'I always say she's like *all* her names. Primrose one minute, Violet the next, Narcissa the next – you can see it all in her eyes. She's several people in one, our Primrose. Of course I don't suppose you see it, but I do.'

Involuntarily Mr Candy looked up, only to be confronted not by the quick chameleon-like beauty of Primrose's eyes but by a fractional glimpse of her bare upper breast, firm and cool as a shell. It unnerved him even more than her eyes' flowery variations.

'I'm sorry, Mr Candy,' Ma suddenly said. 'Would you like something to eat? Bloater paste sandwich or something? Don't think we've got any smoked salmon left today.'

Mr Candy recoiled at the thought of a bloater paste sandwich. 'Thank you, but—'

'*Gentleman's Relish*, then?'

The sound of the words *Gentleman's Relish* in Mr Candy's ears was like nectar. It was an irresistible delight; he went for it bald headed.

'Well, if you really have it—'

'Course,' Ma said. 'We always have it. Never without it.'

'I'm afraid I can't afford it very often.'

'Good. I'll get some made up—'

'No,' Primrose said and there was something sinuous, not at all flower-like, in the way she slipped sideways out of her chair and got up from the table. 'Sit still. I'll get it. You've still got Victoria to do.'

Victoria, though really named after a plum, was blessed with other names that were queen-like. Ma was very much given to queens, especially those, like Marie Antoinette, she could feel sorry for. Accordingly Victoria had also been named Adelaide, another unhappy one, Ann – after the queen who had had eighteen children without any of them surviving, a fact that tore something dreadful at Ma's heartstrings – and Cleopatra. Perhaps because of this burden Victoria was the quietish one of the family. She ate well and all that, as Ma said, but from time to time she was inclined, as Pop said, to go cluck, like hens did.

'Well,' Pop said, 'got the wholesale order wrote out? *En gross*, eh, Mademoiselle Dupont?'

'May I ask a question?' Mademoiselle Dupont said. 'Would the curé perhaps explain my part? I am not to be godmother to *all* the children?'

'Blimey no,' Pop said.

Mr Candy allayed Mademoiselle Dupont's fears by saying that there was nothing to worry about; it was all very simple; and only wished his own could be so easily tranquillised.

On the contrary, several minutes later, they were greatly stimulated, again by the entry of Primrose, carrying a dish of *Gentleman's Relish* sandwiches, nicely decorated by lettuce leaves and tomatoes. Mr Candy felt his mouth water; the evening perhaps hadn't turned out so badly after all. He seized one of the proffered sandwiches with alacrity and started munching, only to discover that in her absence Primrose had changed from her dressing gown into a canary yellow jumper and a green skirt. The jumper seemed at least a size and a half too small for her and produced an effect even more electrifying than the dressing gown, so that he munched in tremulous preoccupation.

'What's all this going to cost me?' Pop suddenly said. He liked to be fair and square and above board in these matters. 'Fair old whack I suppose?'

'Oh! as I told you before, if you remember, there is no charge for baptism, Mr Larkin. Of course if you'd like to make a small contribution to funds for—'

'Course, I remember now. Quid a head be all right?'

Pop said with that bird-like swiftness so greatly charac-
teristic of him. 'Make it ten,' and suddenly tugged from
his pocket a roll of fivers far fatter than a polony sausage,
peeling off two.

Mr Candy was overwhelmed. It was too much. The
desperations of the earlier evening didn't merely dis-
perse; they left in their place a warm, compensatory glow.
It was a joy, almost an exulting one, to be blessed with a
generosity so free and open-handed.

A moment later he was crushed again, this time by
Ma, who said:

'What I did feel, though, Mr Candy, was this. There's
such a big lot of us and it's such a piece-work order for
you and all that I wondered if you wouldn't accept a
little present from me?'

'Oh! my dear Mrs Larkin, there absolutely isn't any
need—'

'It's just a little thing,' Ma said. 'One of my pictures.'

The Rev. Candy felt himself go very cold and very
flaky all over, like a lizard. It was a subject he devoutly
hoped would never come up again. With something like
despair he fairly charged into a *Gentleman's Relish*
sandwich, only to find himself on the verge of half-
choking as Ma said:

'It's one I've done of Primrose. She posed specially.'

Posed? Mr Candy heard himself asking silently. Posed?
The word had a dreadful significance. He could only
remember Mariette.

'Mrs Larkin, you really needn't—'

'Oh! I hope you'll like it,' Ma said. 'Everybody seems

122

to think it's a very good likeness.' Mr Candy quailed, silently. He knew those likenesses. They could explode in your face, he thought, and once again felt himself go very cold and very flaky all over. 'There's a few points I don't like myself. Couldn't quite get the eyes. You know? Anyway, fetch it down, Primrose. It's in our bedroom.'

For the next few minutes Mr Candy wolfed at sandwiches of *Gentleman's Relish* as if they had something medicinal or antidotal about them. He accepted with neither a flicker nor syllable of protest another glass of champagne. He heard himself asking Mademoiselle Dupont in a voice distant and flaky too if she already knew England and heard her echo his own thoughts, rather enigmatically:

'I think there is much that is difficult to know in England.'

Mr Candy thought so too. He could now hear the footsteps of Primrose coming downstairs. They beat with doom at his heart. And then, a few moments later, she was in the room, carrying the picture and Ma was saying:

'Put it somewhere where there's a good light on it, dear. It wants a good light on it.'

Mr Candy actually shut his eyes and saw a vision, before opening them again, of the naked glories of Mariette as seen by Ma. A moment later he found himself looking at a picture of Primrose, in a green jumper and a black skirt, sitting in a chair and modestly holding a small basket of primroses painted in from memory by Ma.

The shock was so great that he felt his body go stiff.

A portion of *Gentleman's Relish* sandwich fell from his fingers. He was suddenly aware of the floor coming up to meet him. He felt colder than ever and a moment later fell forward, as through a black tunnel, on his face, dropping at the feet of Mademoiselle Dupont, who cried '*Quelle horreur!*' and spilled a slow stream of champagne on his face in a final surprising act of baptism, while Ma wondered aloud but imperturbably whatever could have come over him all of a sudden.

9

Ma woke in the night, disturbed by a strange feeling that someone or something was prowling about in the yard outside. She could hear nothing as definite as footsteps and might have let the whole thing slip from her mind as something no more serious than a wakeful turkey if it hadn't been that suddenly she was sure that she heard the clatter of an empty oil drum turning over.

She gave Pop a quick nudge with her elbow in the middle of the back and Pop, who often confessed to having nightmares in which old ladies were chasing him with equally old umbrellas, groaned.

'You awake, Pop?'

Pop said no, he didn't think he was.

'Well, you'd better be. Unless I'm very much mistaken there's somebody prowling about in the yard.'

Pop sleepily wondered who that could be at this time of night and Ma said, rather sharply:

'Poachers, I shouldn't wonder.'

Unperturbed and still more than half asleep Pop wondered aloud who might be poaching and, if so, what?

'Plenty to poach, I should think,' Ma said. 'Geese, turkeys, chickens. Suits of armour—'

'Good Gawd.'

The thought of losing two of his proudest and most treasured possessions made Pop suddenly sit up with an alacrity that surprised even Ma.

'Nobody'd do a thing like that,' he said, 'would they?'

'Oh! wouldn't they?' Ma said. 'They'll nick anything these days. I was reading in the papers only the other day how a gang nicked two great lions from a park. Stone ones, I mean. They weighed a ton apiece or something. You'd better get up and have a peep.'

Pop agreed and got out of bed, stark naked. The experience of sleeping without a stitch of clothing on was one that, in summer, he greatly enjoyed. It compared very favourably with swimming in the never-never, an experience he also enjoyed, quite often, early on summer mornings.

At the bedroom window he half pulled back the curtains and stood looking out. A faint rim of daylight hung over the woods to the east and in the half-light he could just make out the colour of the trees.

'See anything?' Ma said and Pop replied that as far as he could tell everything was as quiet as a church, a remark that by some odd association of ideas reminded Ma of Mademoiselle Dupont.

'You don't suppose it's Mademoiselle by any chance, do you?' she said. 'Sleep-walking or something like that? You never know with these foreigners.'

Pop agreed. Could be. Foreign blood an' all that.

'She's the highly emotional type all right,' Ma said. 'She looked restless all evening, I thought.'

At this remark Pop chuckled deeply.

'Might be out looking for a bit o' stray,' he said.

'Never you mind about looking for a bit of stray,' Ma said, with quite unusual asperity. 'You go down and have a look-see before somebody nicks your suits of armour.'

Pop said he certainly would and turned as if to move to the door.

'Well, not like that, I hope,' Ma said. 'The least you can do is put your trousers on. You don't want to give the poor dear the fright of her life, do you? That would put the tin-lid on it.'

Pop accordingly put on trousers, shirt, socks and slippers and, before going downstairs, told Ma that he somehow didn't think he'd be all that long. It wouldn't surprise him in the least if it wasn't just one of the turkeys. They sometimes got restless too just as dawn was breaking.

'And if it *is* her,' Ma told him firmly, in a final word of warning, 'just remember what I said. Behave. No larking about. It might be misunderstood.'

Pop, after giving the most solemn of promises on this particular matter, went downstairs and into the yard. A few light pools of mist lay over the river and the meadows. Thick white dew, shining as rain, covered the grass. A few birds were stirring and one of his young cockerels, in a comic broken voice, started crowing in a barn.

After being greatly relieved to find that his much-treasured suits of armour were still safely in their places he started strolling about the yard. Everything seemed quiet and normal, he thought, and then suddenly one of his geese started cackling stridently. Instantly every one of his hypersensitive nerves were alert and every instinct warned him that he wasn't alone in the yard.

Somehow he was uncannily sure, also, that he wasn't going to bump into a wandering Mademoiselle Dupont, sleep-walking at dawn. Ma sometimes used the word kipperish to mean something extra fishy and that was how it felt to him now. It felt in fact more than kipperish and the thought made him stop and pick up the broken handle of a hoe that someone had discarded on a muck-heap.

Some few seconds later he heard the sound that Ma had heard: the distinct clatter of an empty oil-drum turning over. It seemed to come from the direction of the hovel where the Rolls was kept and he started walking there.

But less than thirty paces further on he suddenly stopped, convinced that out of the corner of his eye he had seen the flap of a black leather jacket sleeve behind a corner of the barn where his fowls roosted.

He half-walked, half-ran round the side of the barn and suddenly found himself face to face with a girl. She was standing flat against the side of the barn, both hands behind her back. She seemed, he thought, about eighteen or nineteen and was wearing, besides the black leather jacket, tight dark red jeans. Her figure was as flat-chested as a boy's and her face, without a trace of make-up, was a kind of dirty putty colour that threw up into garish relief the big piled-up bee-hive of her hair, the dyed strands of it coarse as string and something of the colour of trampled yellow straw.

'So girls have started poaching now.'

Her lips were thin and colourless and she kept them shut.

'What is it? – chickens, eggs or what?'

He noticed she didn't look at him; instead she kept her eyes on the handle of the hoe.

'What are you up to in my yard?'

'Nothing.'

'Anybody else with you?'

'You got eyes.'

'Don't cheek me. I might warm your backside.'

'You and who else?'

'Don't cheek me.'

She curled her lip.

'Well, you got the big stick. What are you waiting for?'

'What's that you got behind your back?'

'Nothing.'

'Show me.'

She slightly lifted her eyes. They were a cold neutral colour, a sort of rat's tail grey. Otherwise she didn't move and Pop said:

'Show me. Quick.'

'Oh! belt up.'

'What's a kid like you doing out this time o' night?'

'Night? Thought it was day.'

'I said what are you doing in my yard?'

'Well, not chasing an old cock like you, that's for sure.'

'And I said what have you got behind your back?'

'And I said belt up. You put bloody years on me.'

Pop started with anger and moved to grab her arms. She squirmed with steely agility, ducked and slid along the wall. He moved to grab her again but she used the wall of the barn like a spring board and leapt clear away from him by yards. A second later she was racing round the corner of the barn and just as she disappeared Pop saw, for the second time that month, the flash of an open razor.

Some time later he stood so seriously in thought in the bedroom that Ma was moved to ask if he'd seen a ghost or something?

'No.'

'Who was it then?'

'A kid. A girl.'

Ma gave a short laugh and said it was coming to something, wasn't it? Secret meetings at night now, eh? Kidnapping? Pretty?

'Got a razor.'

Oh? Ma inquired. Sort of protecting her honour or something?

'That was summat she never had. The low-down dirty little crawl.'

It wasn't often Pop talked in this vehement way and Ma was perturbed. It was a nice howdedo when girls with razors prowled round your back-yard at night. Next thing they wouldn't even be safe in bed. How did Pop account for a thing like that?

'Search me. It's the way they're dragged up nowadays. Some of 'em, anyway.'

It was almost full daylight by now and Pop still stood

by the window, deep in thought, looking out on the yard, so that presently Ma was prompted to ask him whether or not he was coming back to bed, careful not to frame the question as if it were a direct invitation in case he might not feel in the mood.

Very much to her surprise he didn't. In an absent, preoccupied sort of voice he told her:

'No. Don't think so. I think I'll go and look for mushrooms. It looks like a good mushroom morning to me,' finally adding as an almost melancholy after-thought: 'Well, Ma, we might not have had the kids christened, but at least they growed up a sight better than that dirty little crawl.'

By the time he reached the meadow all trace of mist had cleared. The sun was coming up quickly from behind shoals of fish-shaped clouds, all deep rose except for upper fins of gold. The awnings of the shuttered stalls and roundabouts were damp with the night's dew and he paused for a moment or two to look at them. There was something a trifle sad about a fair by daytime and the sight on this particular morning did nothing to lift his melancholy.

He was still wondering unsuccessfully what a mere kid of a girl could be doing in his yard in the half-dark of the morning with a razor – he felt in some curious way as if he had been cheated, almost betrayed about something – when he became aware of a figure running after him. It was Primrose.

'Ma said you'd gone mushrooming, so I thought I'd come too. Think there'll be any?'

'Caught sight of a few in the distance yesterday but hadn't time to get 'em. You're up early. Restless or something?'

'Couldn't sleep.'

'Summat disturb you?' He was curious to know if she'd heard anything in the night and felt for a moment half-inclined to tell her about the incident of the razor and then decided not to. The whole thing was like a dirty secret. He wouldn't tell another soul.

'Just thoughts.'

Oh! it was like that, was it? he thought to himself and didn't say a word.

'Where was it you saw them yesterday?' she said.

'Over there on the far side o' the medder. Near that big hawthorn.'

Suddenly she stopped and started to take off her shoes and stockings. It was better than getting them soaked with dew, she said. Like Mariette's, her legs were golden brown, almost the same colour and with much the same smooth shine on them as a ripe acorn. She was growing in beauty every day; you could feel maturity possessing her.

When they walked on again her eyes were quick – quick as his own, he thought, perhaps quicker – and it was she who saw the first mushrooms, like a clutch of five white eggs in a patch of longish grass beyond a big straddling hawthorn half-pitched over by some winter gale.

She ran forward to gather them and he followed with a basket. It never failed to excite him to see the first pure whiteness of a new-grown mushroom and the tender salmon of the under-gills when you turned it over. Like the sight of the very first primrose, it made all his veins run faster.

'Beauties,' he said. 'Beauties.'

Her responses were exactly like his own, except that whereas he walked about the field, she ran. The mushrooms were rather few and far between – the season was a bit early, yet – and now and then he found himself tricked by a scrap of sheep's wool, a daisy or a piece of stray paper showing white in the dewy distances.

'This is blowing the cobwebs away,' she said, when they met again. 'I was feeling all frowsy and fuzzy.'

It wasn't doing him any harm either, he thought, and he'd got perhaps a bigger need than she had for a little morning freshness. He didn't suppose anyway that it was anything very serious that had kept her from sleeping and he was half on the point of asking what in fact had kept her awake when she said, in a remarkably secretive sort of way:

'Pop?'

Yes, he said, what was it?

'Know what kept me awake?'

Pop said in his most off-hand way that he hadn't the foggiest.

'Thinking.'

She'd said that before, he reminded her. What had she been thinking about?

'Mr Candy.'

What, he said, made her think about Mr Candy?

'I think I'm in love with him.'

'You *think?*' Pop said and was about to remind her that love was something you couldn't be in two minds about – it either got you by the short hairs or not at all – when she gave him the most melting of glances and said:

'In fact I know I am. I really know.'

Wasn't Mr Candy perhaps a bit old for her? Pop wanted to know, a question to which she replied with an equally direct one of her own:

'How old were you when you fell in love with Ma?'

Oh! about fourteen, Pop supposed.

'You see.'

Exactly how old was Mr Candy anyway? Pop asked her.

'Twenty-four. But age doesn't matter. Age is nothing.'

There was something in that, Pop thought, and stooped to pick two of the most perfick mushrooms he had ever seen: two round sunken shells just moist with dew. The fate of Primrose in the matter of Mr Candy didn't surprise him very much; as he had quite often remarked before it was an extraordinary thing how his daughters, or at least two of them, were inclined to go for the timid type rather than the muscular, he-man sort.

'Does Mr Candy disturb you?' she suddenly said.

Not in any particular way he could think of, Pop said.

'He disturbs me.'

Got under her skin, did he? He knew that feeling all right. Angela Snow gave it to him sometimes.

'No, it isn't that,' she said. 'I just feel there's a lot we don't know about him. I feel he's a bit mysterious.'

That hadn't struck him at all, Pop said. Mr Candy mysterious? How?

'Can't really explain. But he used to work in a parish in the East End of London and he's a bit cagey about it. All rather strange, I think.'

Pop suddenly laughed and made the pronouncement that you could hardly expect anything else with parsons. They were a rum lot. Comical, he thought.

'Oh! Mr Candy's not comical. I don't think so, anyway. I think there's a side to him none of us have ever seen yet. It'll come out one day.'

That was what you called feminine tuition or summat, Pop supposed. Women were clever, really, the way they saw through you. No foxing 'em. What other side of Mr Candy could possibly be revealed? he wondered. All he saw was a timid young man as nervous of girls and company in general as a new-born pup. Nothing hidden, nothing mysterious about him at all.

'I think we've just about cleared the field,' he said. He thought the mushrooms in the basket probably weighed less than a pound but they were clean and fresh and would make a couple of good breakfasts. 'Shall we go back? Feet cold?'

'Oh! no. Lovely. Washed in dew. Better than a bath.'

Washed in dew, Pop thought. That just about described

it. He suddenly drew in large exquisite breaths of morning air and looked down with paternal fondness at the young pretty brown feet walking through the wet summer grass. In return Primrose looked up at him and smiled slowly, with a slight hint of indulgence, as if she saw through him too.

The smile dispelled the last of his uneasiness of mind. As they walked the rest of the distance to the house he felt more and more as if washed in dew himself and that the incident in the night might never have happened.

Pop normally ate two breakfasts, one a mere snack designed temporarily to stave off the first morning pangs at about six o'clock, the second, his proper breakfast, at somewhere between eight and half past; but today the incident of the girl with the razor and then that of Primrose and the mushrooms had caused him, surprisingly, to skip the first completely. Still more surprisingly he found himself not over-hungry at eight o'clock and was content to toy with a mere half dozen rashers of bacon and a plate of mushrooms.

While he was eating these Mr Charlton arrived in the kitchen and Pop greeted him with a 'Morning, Charley boy' which, rather low in tone, lacked much of his customary clarion sprightliness.

Mr Charlton, at Pop's instigation, had lately taken up the pheasant chick lark and it was turning out to be a very paying game. You got a very nice price for the chicks, which by the time they were full grown and roaming the autumn stubbles would cost the shooters not less than a tenner a time. It all seemed sheer folly to Pop, who couldn't blame the gypsies for frequently poaching half of them with gin-soaked raisins.

'Morning, Pop,' Mr Charlton said. 'You sound a trifle under the weather.'

'I fancy he is too,' Ma said.

'Haven't let the police-court get on your mind, have you?'

'Good Gawd, the police-court! It's Friday. Ma, I forgot every word about it. It's the day Edith and the General and me have to go and give evidence. Gawd strike me pink, I forgot.'

At the recollections of the police-court Pop's spirits seemed suddenly to drop again. The prospect of wasting half a summer day kicking his heels in court simply appalled him.

'Gawd, Charley boy, I got a million things to do. Any idea how long they might keep us there?'

'I'd deal with 'em in five minutes, the hooligans,' Ma said, 'if I had my way. And no half larks. I'd cut their livers and lights out. Cold.'

'It all depends,' Mr Charlton said.

'On what?' Pop said.

With precise and expert smoothness Mr Charlton at once proceeded to explain, while Pop listened marvelling, open-mouthed, that it all depended on which type of offence had been committed. In all probability the two accused would plead not guilty, reserve their defence and elect to be tried by jury at the Assizes or Quarter Sessions.

'Good Gawd.'

'There are in fact three types of offence of this nature,' Mr Charlton airily went on to explain. 'Under *The Offences Against The Person Act* 1861, *Section* 18 *and again Sections* 20 *and* 47—'

Pop felt himself recoil under the sheer brilliant weight of Mr Charlton's expert words. You certainly had to hand it to Charley. He wondered where he got it from. There were no flies of any kind on Charley boy.

'My impression,' Mr Charlton said, 'is that they will be committed to the next quarter sessions or assizes, where you'll have to give evidence. The whole thing, I should say, will come under *Section* 18 of the Act, for which in fact these jokers can get imprisonment for life.'

'Never?'

'Good egg!' Ma said. 'And a good horse-whipping too.'

'In any case you shouldn't be there very long today. By the way, which car are you taking? The Jag or the Rolls?'

Pop said he thought the Rolls; Edith was so fond of it. Why did Charley ask?

'I'll wash it over for you if you like,' Mr Charlton said. 'I've got nothing much to do.'

'Very nice of you, Charley boy. Very nice of you. Just once over lightly.'

'Finish your breakfast in peace. I'll get on with it right away,' Mr Charlton said and went out into the yard.

Less than five minutes later he was back again, more than slightly agitated, to inform an astonished Pop that he somehow didn't think he'd be going to court in either the Jag or the Rolls after all.

'Why?' Pop said. 'How's that then?'

'You'll be needing ten new tyres for a start. Every one's been slashed. With a razor I should say.'

Ma instantly gave a loud, irreverent snort and said it fair made you want to spit.

'Your poaching little crawl in the night,' she said. 'Want me to come along as body-guard? Unless I'm very much mistaken you'll be needing a bit of protection one of these fine days.'

'The Rolls!' was all Pop could say. 'The Rolls! To do a thing like that to the Rolls!'

Pop was back home for a late lunch, having stopped on the way to fortify himself, the Brigadier and Edith Pilchester with several large and much-needed brandies at *The Hare & Hounds*.

'Well,' Ma said, 'tell me about it. What happened? Put 'em away for a good long spell?'

No, Pop proceeded to explain, it was just exactly like Charley boy had said – you really had to hand it to Charley – they were both remanded on bail to appear at the next Assizes.

'Looked about as arrogant as a pair o' Nazis. I thought one of 'em 'd spit in the Clerk o' the Court's eye.'

'Disgusting.'

'How did poor old Edith take it?'

Pop said he thought Edith was really frightened; he

was worried about Edith, living in that cottage of hers all alone.

'Tell her about the girl and the razor?'

Pop confessed that he hadn't; he was honestly afraid to, in case it might make her more frightened still.

'But you'll have to tell the police?'

'Going back there this afternoon.'

Ma then proceeded to ask about the Brigadier. How had the Brigadier shaped up to it all?

'Well,' Pop said, 'it was rather funny in a way, about the General. He turned up sort of all dressed up and on parade. Best suit, rolled umbrella, gold watch-chain and bowler hat. Looked ready to defend the Right and the Faith and all that.'

Here Pop paused to give a sprightly and passable imitation of the Brigadier defending the Right and the Faith with his rolled umbrella. It failed, surprisingly, to make Ma laugh.

'Not that he'd stand much chance with them birds. They'd cut their own grandmother up for cats' meat.'

For a moment Ma seemed about to utter a typical expression of disgust but instead she grew unexpectedly pensive. Though she couldn't yet bring herself to confess it to Pop, she too was frightened. One day everything in the garden was lovely; the next there was poison in the air.

At that moment Pop, intuitively sensing that she was ill-at-ease, put a consolatory arm round her enormous waist and asked if she wouldn't join him in a Red Bull, his favourite cocktail?

140

'I will an' all,' she said. 'And you can mix it up good and strong and quadruple into the bargain. I need it bad.'

'Not worried, Ma?'

To this Ma had no answer to give until Pop had put into her hands the largest Red Bull even she had ever seen – Pop remarked that it was a real pepper-upper – when she said:

'I don't mind telling you I am. What's more, if this goes on you'll have to start keeping your shot gun by your bedside.'

Pop, after gravely taking a good, deep gulp of Red Bull, slowly shook his head.

'Can't do that, Ma.'

What did he mean? Ma wanted to know. Couldn't do what?

'What you said. I already asked Charley boy about it. Can't take up fire-arms to use against jokers like these breaking in at night. Musn't use no more force than is reasonable. Charley says so. And Charley knows.'

Ma, in great disgust, took an almost savage swig at her Red Bull.

'What are we supposed to resist 'em with, then? Spoons?'

Pop rather gloomily confessed he didn't know. But that, according to Charley boy, was how it was.

'What are we all coming to?' Ma suddenly demanded to know in a positive flame of passion fed by yet another furious swig at the Red Bull. 'Where in the name of all the saints are we supposed to be? England? I sometimes begin to doubt it.'

Pop had half begun to doubt it himself and was presently further shattered by Ma thrusting an empty glass into his hands.

'Here, give me a re-fill, do. A good big one an' all. My faith needs a bit of restoring today.'

10

On Sunday morning, while the Larkins were uncon-
cernedly breakfasting on their customary fried eggs,
bacon, sausages, mushrooms, tomatoes and fried bread,
with much ketchup, Mademoiselle Dupont stayed late
in bed, sipping weak tea, which she regarded more as
a medicine than anything, and munching on dry toast
and honey. Though the duty lying before her was really
a light one she still viewed it with alarm and a tension
springing from nerves frayed from the dismaying
experiences of two days before.

Ma and Pop had held brief court on these alarms and
tensions, in bed, the night before.

'Bundle of nerves, you can see that,' Ma said. 'Hardly
eats anything either. Jumpy as a kitten.'

Pop agreed, but nevertheless, recalling the Brigadier's
trenchant words on the subject, had a simple explanation.
Foreign blood.

'Suppose so,' Ma said. 'You've been behaving yourself,
though, Syd Larkin, I hope, haven't you?'

'Not kissed her yet,' Pop said, as if this interesting
experience might have provided a solution to Mademoiselle Dupont's emotional crisis. 'Suppose I ought?'

Ma said she thought it would be a far better idea
if he drove Mademoiselle to church in the buggy. It

would be a more tranquillising experience than the Rolls.

'Might make Edith jealous,' Pop said.

'You and your women,' Ma said. 'Why don't you start a harem?'

'Strength's a very fine thing,' Pop said and Ma, laughing with spontaneous splendour, gave him an affectionate wallop in the back.

Mr Candy was another very bad case of nerves, she went on to say. She sometimes didn't know what to make of Mr Candy. She could only suppose it was living alone and all that. Not having anybody to share things with.

'By the way,' Pop said, 'Primrose's in love with him.'

'Oh! really?' Ma said. 'Not surprised.'

'And she was telling me too how he used to work in an East End parish in London,' Pop said. 'Very like that accounts for something.'

Ma said she shouldn't wonder. It was more than likely. London was no good to anybody. It was good enough to unmoralise you. Give her the country any day.

'Talking about unmoralising,' she went on, 'is it next week you have to go and give evidence at the Assizes about them two hooligans?'

'No, the next.'

'Pity. I must say I'll be glad when it's over.'

Mademoiselle Dupont, rising at last between eleven and half-past, found herself facing the first problem of the day. It was whether to wear Pop's tantalising gift of black lingerie or to settle for something more modest and substantial? The experience of wearing so intimately personal a gift would hardly make for serenity, yet the least she felt she could do was to wear it, so to speak, in honour of the day.

At last she put the garments on, only to find herself quivering so much that she immediately took them off again, replacing them with plainer and more honest things, the lower of which she secured, in case of possible accident, with two enormous safety pins.

She then took four aspirins, finished putting on her plain black dress with white sleeve and collar pipings, her black and white hat and her white gloves. Finally she crossed herself several times, said a short prayer and bathed her forehead in eau-de-cologne.

Going downstairs at twenty minutes to twelve, she found most of the Larkins ready. Ma was wearing a dress of mauve chiffon, with a large picture hat decorated all over with violets and pink daisies. Pop was in a remarkably subdued suit of clerical grey, with a large red clove carnation in the buttonhole. The christening lark had got to be treated with a bit of seriousness, he had finally decided, whatever goings-on might happen later, when grub and totting out and all that started.

The twins, all in white except for the distinguishing scarlet and purple ribbons in their hair, seemed to Mademoiselle Dupont like a pair of little angels. They reminded her so much of the young girls one saw in those lovely confirmatory processions back home in Brittany. The sweetest, most angelic things.

'Well, it's going uphill for twelve,' Ma said. 'Where's Primrose? Everybody's ready except Primrose.'

'Still making up,' Victoria said.

Victoria was in palest blue, a colour that gave her a certain visionary serenity.

'Better nip up and tell her to hurry,' Ma said. 'Oh! do be quiet, little Oscar. You'll drown the living daylights out of us.'

Little Oscar was sitting in a chair at the table, which he was loudly and vigorously banging with one of Ma's wooden spoons. He was wearing a light cream tussore suit which threw up into shining relief his fat red moon of a face, which seemed almost beery in its healthiness.

'Oh! go to Mademoiselle Dupont for a minute, do.' Ma instantly plonked the well-stuffed shape of Oscar into Mademoiselle Dupont's unready arms, so that she almost staggered as she clasped him with a sudden rush of Gallic affection to her deep firm bosom. 'Go to your godmother.'

'*Ah! mon chérie! Chérie! – tchook, tchook, tchook!*'

'Nice an' warm in 'ere!' little Oscar said, using one of his favourite expressions.

Presently, with Primrose still nowhere to be seen, Mr Charlton, Mariette and little Blenheim arrived. Mr Charlton too was wearing a charcoal grey suit with a dark red rose in his buttonhole and to Ma's infinite astonishment was carrying a black bowler and a black rolled umbrella. Altogether Ma thought he looked so posh that she half-wished Pop had sported a bowler too.

She'd a good mind to buy him one for Christmas – perhaps one in green or brown.

Mademoiselle Dupont gazed at Mr Charlton with inexpressible rapture. He, at any rate, with his *melon*, his *sang-froid* and his umbrella, epitomised the England of her dreams. Here at last was the true, real Englishman.

Mariette, who looked a model of sheer allurement in a white silk suit and a white birthday cake of a hat with many buttercup flowers springing up all over it, suddenly said:

'Personally I think we ought to get started. Mr Candy'll be having an accident or something if we keep him waiting.'

'Quite right,' Pop said. 'Time's getting on. Charley boy, you take the Rolls and load up. I'll bring Mademoiselle Dupont and Primrose in the buggy. Where is that gal? Snifter afore you go, Charley?'

'No snifters!' Ma said with a firmness almost unparalleled at that particular time of Sunday morning, when she and Pop would normally have been sharing snifters by the dozen, 'we don't want the church to pong like a four-ale bar.'

With the newly tyred Rolls moving sweetly out of the yard and little Oscar waving his wooden spoon out of the back window Pop found himself presently caught between the dual temptation of the cocktail cabinet and Mademoiselle Dupont. He couldn't quite decide whether to give Mademoiselle Dupont a couple of rapid nerve-soothers or to mix himself a quick Red Bull in spite of Ma.

He was saved from the necessity of making this excruciating decision by the serene arrival, at ten minutes past twelve, of Primrose. Her make-up, though by no means obtrusive, had taken her well over an hour and now had the effect of making her look all of nineteen. Her dress, quite low at the neck and very short-sleeved, was exactly of the right primrose colour to match her name. The belt round her waist was broad and in emerald green and gave her a high up-lifted bust. Her gloves were of the same colour as her hat and threw into relief the deep sallow colour of her arms. Her hat was the merest spider's web of green lace and looked as if it had dropped on to her rich black hair with the morning dew.

Even Pop was stunned. He vaguely murmured something about 'Ready?' and had neither the heart nor will to scold her for lateness. He'd always said she'd be the *belle* of the family; he wasn't sure she wasn't even lovelier than Mariette. She even approached his vision of an earlier Ma, splendid in her own precocious maturity.

Impressed too, Mademoiselle Dupont gave an enchanted sigh and two minutes later the three of them were driving away in the buggy, to a jingle of bells, into a morning from which the muggy vapours of July were at last lifting, to let the sun come through.

The Rev. Candy had not merely had one accident that morning, but several. First he had cut himself an uncountable number of times while shaving, so that for a time he had gone about with bits of white cotton-wool sticking out all over his face, rather like a tattered Christmas party snowman. Then out of sheer anxiety he had mistaken the time and had arrived at the church at a quarter to eleven instead of a quarter to twelve. There was no morning service, so that for an hour he had been obliged to sit alone in the vestry, until finally deciding to make himself a cup of instant coffee, which through impossible nervousness he promptly spilled down the front of his trousers.

When he finally emerged from the vestry he got the immediate impression that there were far more people gathered about the christening font, on which a number of candles were burning, than he or the Rev. Spinks ever saw at a service.

Nor, he thought, had he ever been confronted with quite such an array of beauty. To the collective allurements of the Larkin family were now added the ravishments of Jasmine Brown and Angela Snow. Like a cool but hardly blessed pair of sirens, one brunette, one blonde, they stood together, radiating a strange compulsive sort of calm. Miss Pilchester was also there, wearing a rather outdated purple pork-pie of a hat, which Ma slowly recognised as one she had long since sent to a jumble sale.

'Good morning to you all,' the Rev. Candy said. His voice was low though not appreciably nervous. He was determined to keep an iron hand on himself, come what might. 'Well, I think we might commence if everyone is here.'

'Just waiting for Mr Larkin and Primrose and Mademoiselle Dupont,' said Ma, who was jogging little Oscar gently up and down. 'I thought I heard the buggy draw up just now.'

This unexpected delay in the programme caused Mr Candy to draw a hard breath and go cold and flaky again. He shifted his book of service from hand to hand and tugged nervously at his vestments.

A moment or two later the three late-comers entered the church. Instantly a kind of disquieting radiance fell on the scene. Primrose might have been a flame burning her way down the nave and Mr Candy, as she gave him the most direct of smiles, felt himself quail as he had never quailed before.

For some inexplicable reason he took refuge in humour. A solemn joke sprang from his lips before he could stop it.

'Has everyone his or her little book giving the form of service? And is everyone now familiar with the batting order?'

Conscious as they all were of being in church, nobody laughed, and in the succeeding hush Mr Candy felt abysmally ashamed.

'Little Blenheim's first,' Ma said.

'Who is to be the god-parent of this child?'

Angela Snow said she was and succeeded, as she stepped forward a pace, in looking ravishingly demure.

'Oscar Larkin is next, I believe. Who is the god-parent of this child?'

'I. Mademoiselle Dupont.'

'Step this way, please.'

Angela Snow, Mademoiselle Dupont and the Rev. Candy retired some distance from the font and went for some moments into solemn conclave. In the resulting hush the only sounds that could be heard were the shrillings of swallows and sparrows above the roof outside and an occasional cough from the Brigadier, who had discreetly taken up a strategic guard position some distance down the nave.

The service presently began. Little Blenheim, being not only very tiny but also fast asleep, presented no difficulty and lay sweetly swaddled and oblivious in Mr Candy's arms while Mr Candy poured unnecessarily large quantities of water over the back of his minute bald head, so that Ma was quite disgusted and said under her breath:

'Here, don't drown the child in the drink, for goodness' sake.'

Mercifully Mr Candy didn't drown little Blenheim in the drink but gave him back to Mariette and then turned his attention to little Oscar. Little Oscar, not by any means all that little now, was a great weight in his arms. Mr Candy could hardly hold him. Oscar was also very restless and with his red cherubic face looked not at all unlike a slightly inebriated piglet struggling about.

'I baptise this child Oscar Columbus Septimus Dupont,' Mr Candy said, hoping to heaven that he had the names right and at the same time slopping more unnecessarily large quantities of water over Oscar's head.

Almost immediately afterwards Oscar, who had insisted on bringing Ma's wooden spoon to church with him – and why not? Ma said, if it would keep the child pacified – struck Mr Candy a severe blow on the top of the head with it. Mr Candy recoiled in pain.

The twins instantly giggled and even Mademoiselle Dupont could hardly suppress a laugh. Little Oscar actually laughed too, in the form of a delighted crow, and Ma whispered under her breath:

'Oscar! Remember where you are.'

In reply Oscar, having greatly enjoyed the experience of striking Mr Candy once, now proceeded to strike him a second time, but rather more severely. Mr Candy instinctively ducked and the sound of the wooden spoon cracking down on his skull was distinctly hollow.

'Nice an' warm in 'ere!' Oscar said.

'Here, give him back to me,' Ma said and Mr Candy promptly did so, with undisguised relief and a faint smile that seemed to indicate that he was quite used to this sort of thing.

Instantly Oscar, rudely deprived of the pleasure of using Mr Candy's head as a drum, burst loudly into tears, with the result that Ma had hastily to take him out of church, where she promptly pacified him with a large Bath bun she had thoughtfully popped into her handbag in case of such an emergency. Little Oscar dried up at once. There was nothing like a bit of grub, Ma thought, for stopping that sort of nonsense.

Confused by the unexpected attack on him, Mr Candy now discovered that he had forgotten the batting order and began searching in his trousers' pocket for the little book in which he'd written it down, only to discover that the book was sliding slowly down his trousers' leg. The hole in his pocket was one he had been meaning to mend for a month or more.

The result of this was that he called Montgomery next and Montgomery, being covered in adolescent masculine shyness as opposed to the serene aplomb of the girls, hastily stepped forward, only too glad to get the ordeal over. He was shortly followed by Mariette, who treated the occasion with such grace and dignity, together with a complete detachment, that Mr Charlton felt a great lump of pride rise in his throat.

Pop, on the other hand, thought Mr Candy was holding Mariette's head far too near the candles. He didn't want to see any of his kids go up in smoke and him having to act as fireman or anythink of that lark, and he was almost constrained to tell Mr Candy as much when to his relief he saw Mariette walking back to Mr Charlton. At one point in the service he couldn't help thinking there was a dickens of a lot of water slopping about but perhaps it was just as well after all.

During all this Primrose kept her eyes firmly fixed on Mr Candy, who was deeply and hopelessly conscious of it all the time. The beautiful dark stare had him in a celestial vice. There was no escaping it and even when he stooped down to pick up the little book containing the batting order he could feel its silent penetration at the back of his head.

Some knowledge of the batting order was now essential because of the twins. That simply had to be right and Mr Candy hastily refreshed his memory about their names and ribbon colours. Zinnia would be wearing the red ribbon and Petunia the purple.

The twins now stepped meekly forward and, white and innocent as milk, stood by the font. You couldn't tell them apart. They might have been two identical cherubs cut in stone.

'Let us see,' Mr Candy said to Petunia, 'you are Petunia, with the purple ribbon.'

'No,' Petunia said. 'I'm Zinnia.'

'But you're wearing the purple ribbon.'

'I know. But we changed.'

'Zinnia is supposed to be wearing scarlet. Isn't that right?'

'Yes,' Zinnia said, 'but Petunia hates purple.'

'So Zinnia is now wearing purple and Petunia scarlet?'

'That's right,' they said almost together, 'would you like us to change back again?'

Suddenly, to his horror, Mr Candy found himself in what Ma would have called a terrible two-and-eight. He simply didn't know where he was. Desperately he recalled Ma's words about the mischief-loving nature of the twins and just as desperately looked round for some help and succour from Ma. But Ma was still outside, feeding Bath bun to little Oscar, and Mr Candy could only turn his extreme desperation on the twins.

'Now you are quite sure about this? You wouldn't want me to give you the wrong names, would you?'

'Would it matter?'

'Of course it would matter.'

'Well, I think we changed ribbons three times, but I'm not sure,' Petunia said. 'We had a bit of a tiff. Because I don't like purple.'

'*You* don't like purple – Oh! my Heaven, this is awfully awkward,' Mr Candy said and with fresh desperation turned to Pop. 'Mr Larkin, can you tell me which girl is which? I must be sure.'

'Search me, old man,' Pop said, 'they're more alike some days than others. Ma's the one what knows. You'll have to get Ma.'

'I'll fetch her,' Mariette said.

Still fixing Mr Candy with that dark, celestial stare of hers, Primrose said in a slow soft voice:

'Zinnia has a mole. You'd know if you found that.'

Mr Candy's already carroty hair seemed suddenly to turn several deeper shades of ginger. Nervously he jerked his vestments about, so that the candle flames waved.

'What's all this?' Ma said.

'We've run into some difficulty, Mrs Larkin,' Mr Candy said. 'Can you please tell me which twin is which?'

'That's Petunia,' Ma said promptly, pointing to Zinnia, 'and that's Zinnia,' she said, pointing to Petunia. 'That's right, isn't it?'

The twins, who hitherto had been straight-faced, now merely smirked.

'Are you two wearing the right ribbons?' Ma said.

'They say they changed,' Mr Candy started to say, only to be promptly interrupted by Ma, who now had doubts of her own and said she'd be blowed if she was certain after all.

'Nothing for it but to have a look,' she said, seizing the twin she thought was Zinnia by the head and hastily taking her behind the red vestry curtains.

While this was going on Primrose gave Mr Candy a slow smile of sheer honey, which he involuntarily half-returned and which she repeated, infinitely more slowly, when Ma came back and said:

'Sorry, Mr Candy. This is Petunia. I'll warm their bottoms when I get them home.'

The twins, once again indivisible in heavenly, milky innocence, didn't turn a hair and merely waited for the blessing of baptism in patient silence, as if wondering what all the fuss was about.

After these nervous difficulties the task of christening Victoria Adelaide Anne Cleopatra would have been an infinitely simple one if it hadn't been for the flame that was Primrose. Somehow Mr Candy knew he was going to burn his fingers there. Feeling very flaky and very cold all over again, he could only pray silently for a quick and merciful delivery.

Then when Primrose at last came forward to the font, her green-gloved hands lightly clasped in front of her, he discovered to his immense surprise that she did so with a modesty almost touching. The smile had gone from her face. Her large dark eyes were solemn. He suddenly felt that the two of them were alone in the church and that her beauty might have been that of a bride.

Finally as she raised and then lowered her head over the font, he touched her for the first time and as the holy water dropped on her forehead he said:

'I baptize you Primrose, Violet, Anemone, Iris, Magnolia, Narcissus.'

'Narcissa,' she whispered, 'you silly.'

He was too confused to grasp whether the words were of reproval or affection, but when he had finally corrected himself and she had lifted her head again she gave him the benefit of the most forgiving and disarming of smiles. And this, accompanied as it was by the embarrassingly distinct sound of low sobbing from Mademoiselle Dupont, unnerved him so much that he actually knocked one of the candles over and only just saved it from dropping into holy water.

Twenty minutes later he was standing in the marquee with Pop, who was clapping him on the back with extreme jollity and saying:

'Very well done, old man. Very enjoyable. You umpired well. Very good umpire. Calls for a drink, eh?'

Mr Candy could only think it called for several drinks.

'What'll it be, old man, eh? Whisky, gin, rum, brandy, champagne?'

Mr Candy said if it was all the same to Pop he'd prefer a small whisky.

Pop turned smartly away and came back a fraction of a minute later with two and a half inches of whisky in a tumbler and a glass of champagne for himself. The marquee was now filling rapidly with people; dresses and beauty floated everywhere. There was a smell of food and bruised grass and with pride Pop urged Mr Candy to cast his peepers on a vast board laden with cold turkey, duck, chicken, ham, tongue, salmon, green seas of water-cress and salad, scores of bottles and many red-and-snowy dishes of strawberries and cream.

'Very proud day, this,' Pop said, raising his glass, 'for me and Ma. Thanks, old man.'

Mr Candy raised his glass too and drank and then found himself some few moments later alone in the world for the second time that morning with Primrose, who greeted him with words that fell on him like a sweet and final benediction.

'Thank you,' she said, holding him with that slow dark smile of hers, 'you did it so beautifully.'

'Thank you, Narcissa,' he said, also with a smile, and knew that for the first time in several weeks he was happy.

11

By mid afternoon the sun was shining brilliantly from a sky broken by occasional high white sails of cloud. A clear candescent light lay everywhere and Ma, her easel set up in the shade of the walnut tree, was busy sketching in the gay scene of marquee, flags, roundabout, swings and all, determined to preserve it for what she sometimes called prosperity.

Miss Pilchester, with the twins, was strenuously hurling balls at coconuts; Mademoiselle Dupont had retired to her room ostensibly to sleep but in reality to shed a few quiet, happy tears. Montgomery was working the roundabout for a dozen children or more, among them little Oscar who, inseparable from his wooden spoon was banging the head of the cockerel he was riding even more fiercely then he had banged that of Mr Candy. Pop and Mr Candy, in shirt sleeves, were in the kitchen with Angela Snow, Primrose and Jasmine Brown, all washing up, Pop now and then pausing to pay caressive attention to Angela and Jasmine and occasionally warmly urging Mr Candy to follow suit. Mr Candy, however, was firm in refusal. He had, he thought, had quite enough emotional exercise for one day.

As Pop was drying the last of the dishes he suddenly

put to Mr Candy, in his quick swallow-like way, one of those inconsequential questions of his:

'Anybody poor in the village nowadays, Mr Candy? I mean real poor. Poor and hungry.'

Mr Candy, caught unawares, pondered briefly before answering, and then said no, he honestly didn't think so. Times had changed.

'Telling me,' Pop said. He recalled the days when the village shop had little to offer but candles, tea, paraffin, lard and cuts of rough old bacon. Now every Tom, Dick and Harry rolled up for scampi, smoked salmon and fancy larks of that sort.

'Why do you ask?' Mr Candy said.

'Plenty of cold turkey left,' Pop said, recalling that Ma had cooked four big ones, 'and I was just wondering if you could think of anybody who'd like a chunk or two.'

Mr Candy, who couldn't help thinking that he wouldn't mind a chunk or two himself, said:

'There's old Mrs Francis. She lives alone. I fancy she doesn't often see such luxuries.'

'Good egg,' Pop said. There were the little Miss Barnwells too, Effie and Edna; he often fancied that they lived, as Ma said, on bread-and-scrat. Perhaps Mr Candy wouldn't mind taking them some too?

'Gladly. Gladly.'

'Then let's go over and a do a bit of disjointing. Don't go away, girls. Be back in no time.'

'We're going to put our swimsuits on,' Jasmine said.

160

'Why bother?' Pop said blandly, at the same time running a strategic hand over the fuller, rounder parts of the girl, certain that she had little if anything on underneath her thin silk dress. 'Anybody want unzipping?'

On this flippant note he and Mr Candy walked across to the marquee, merely pausing for a silent second or two on the way to admire Miss Pilchester, who was winding and unwinding with an almost masculine ferocity as she hurled frequent balls at coconuts. It was all very gay, all very perfick, Pop thought. He loved especially the laughter of kids from the roundabout and the way the organ tunes – the old *Gold & Silver* waltz, Ma's favourite, was the one playing at the moment – fairly danced on the air. You couldn't hardly find anythink more perfick, or more peaceful, nowhere.

In the marquee Pop started to disjoint, with his fingers, the three quarter remains of a twelve-pound turkey, frequently popping morsels of stuffing into his mouth and also genially suggesting that Mr Candy should help himself at the beer keg if he had a mind.

Mr Candy, though grateful, said no, he'd rather not. A few glasses of champagne had made him very thirsty. What he'd honestly really like was a glass of water.

'Good God,' Pop said. 'Water?' It didn't seem possible. Was Mr Candy feeling dicky?

'No. Merely thirsty. It's the champagne.'

'That's what Ma always says. Just a good excuse for drinking more, I always say.'

There was, as it turned out, no water but Mr Candy

found a jug of lemonade and poured himself a glass of that.

With this in his hands he stood watching Pop doing deft work with the turkey when suddenly, out of the corner of his eye, he was aware of two figures standing at the door of the tent, each in black sweater, stove-pipe trousers and winkle-pickers, the taller of the two also wearing a red shoe-string necktie.

'I think you have visitors, Mr Larkin,' he said.

Pop turned sharply, paused in the act of halving a turkey leg and merely said:

'Ah! the big brave boys.'

Mr Candy slowly set his glass of lemonade on the table.

'Look who's here, Jed. Palsy-walsy Larkin and parson's nose. Lemonade boy.'

'What do you two want?' Pop said. 'Buzz. I'm busy.'

'Nobody don't mean nothing unfriendly, do they Jed? We just 'eard you 'ad a party.'

No, Jed said, nobody didn't mean nothing unfriendly. How could they, with parson's nose here?

'No, not with clergy-wergy about. Wouldn't be nice. Not with clergy-wergy pudden an' pie.'

Mr Candy didn't move at all as the two men advanced across the tent and Pop merely picked up another leg of turkey.

'Nothing a bit unfriendly. Only wanted to make a little social call. By the way, palsy-walsy, where's the old trout?'

'Yeh, where's the old trout? The old coconut trout, we

mean. Got to 'ave a word with 'er, see? Got to trim 'er nails a bit, see?'

'Ah! get lost,' Pop said. The sudden mention of Edith Pilchester made him fearful and he crooked an angry elbow. 'Go and drown yourself. Quick.'

'Now, now. Now, now. Temper. And where's Tweedledum? We got to 'ave a word with Tweedledum too, see? Old pink-cap, we mean, see?'

'Yeh, got to 'ave a word with everybody, see? Old mother coconut, pink-cap and palsy-walsy. The lot. On account of we don't want no trouble in court, see? Don't want to 'ave nobody saying nothing they don't mean, like, see?'

Pop, trembling now with anger, shook a turkey leg in the air like a threatening club.

'Now I give you jokers just ten seconds—'

'Don't you wave no bony-wony at me, palsy-walsy boy. Else I might make pretty patterns on your kiss-woz, see?'

Pop saw Jed whip a hand into his inside jacket pocket but before he himself could move Mr Candy stepped forward.

'I suggest you go,' he said, 'unless you want me as a further unfriendly witness.'

''Ark who's talking! 'Ark who's unfriendly. Old parson's nose. Old clergy-wergy.'

'I merely—'

'Keep your big mouth shut, clergy-wergy. Belt up.'

'Unless you want me to shut it for you,' Jed said. 'What say?'

'Oh! you shut it,' Mr Candy said with great politeness. 'It's so much easier.'

'I bloody well will an' all!'

A second later Jed aimed a cruncher at Mr Candy's jaw but Mr Candy, with an alacrity so smart that Pop had never been more surprised in his life, ducked smartly and was astonishingly revealed ready for instant action as a southpaw.

'Cut him to bacon-rind, Jed!'

'Your move,' Mr Candy said. 'Come on.'

Jed came on, two fisted, and a moment later Pop had the second surprise of his life. Mr Candy suddenly had a half-nelson on Jed so well-locked that any moment Pop expected to hear the crack of a bone.

'Shall I break it?' Mr Candy said. 'Won't take a second.'

Jed started to yell in vicious pain.

'Knock him off! Knock him off!'

'Call your whippet off,' Mr Candy said. 'Or I'll break it.'

'God, you parson bastard!'

In answer Mr Candy put another ounce or two of pressure on the half-nelson. Jed screamed in wild agony.

'You're not even chicken,' Mr Candy said. 'You're just the white of the egg.'

'Let me go! Let me go!'

To Pop's infinite astonishment Mr Candy let him go.

'Now scramble,' he said. 'Scramble. Pronto. Or next time I'll break it. I'll break both of them.'

Only a moment or two later Mr Candy and Pop were

alone in the tent, Pop so astounded that for once in his life he was completely speechless. He simply couldn't think of a thing to say. He even went so far as to do another utterly unprecedented thing by picking up Mr Candy's glass of lemonade and taking a long, sharp swig at it. By God, he'd go to Jericho. He'd ruddy well go to Jericho.

'Did a fair bit of it at one time,' Mr Candy said. 'Had to. At the club. I broke a bone once. Nasty sound. I thought perhaps I might have been a little out of practice.'

At this moment Pop, still utterly speechless, could think only of the sharer of all his secrets, Ma. He simply had to tell Ma. He simply had to! and with a sort of hunting cry he rushed from the marquee, leaving Mr Candy in a mood of what seemed to be quiet reflection, helping himself at the beer-keg.

Ma, rather to Pop's surprise, was no longer at her easel and he could only guess that she'd gone upstairs for a lay-down. He profoundly hoped so anyway. In that case he could kill two birds with one stone.

He went upstairs and, so excited by events that all thought even of Jasmine Brown had gone from his mind, hastily opened the bedroom door, poked his head in and said:

'Ma, my little old sunflower. You there?'

Ma was there, tucked up in bed, a bottle of aspirins and a glass of water standing on the table at the bedside. Pop stood greatly astonished. He could think of only one good reason why Ma should come to bed on a Sunday afternoon and it had nothing to do with aspirins.

'All right, my old sunflower? Not feeling dicky?'

Ma, he couldn't help thinking, looked a tiny bit pale round the gills.

'Just tired.'

'Long day. Too much excitement. Upset you to tan the twins too, I expect?'

'Didn't tan them after all. Hadn't the heart.'

Ma sounded sort of limp, Pop thought, and urgently asked if he couldn't get her a drop of something – brandy, port, rum or perhaps a cocktail?

Ma shook her head and refused without a word, so that Pop was compelled to ask if she'd had one of her turns?

'No. Nothing like that,' Ma said. 'I probably shouldn't have started painting. But I wanted to get it down as a sort of memento.'

Pop suddenly sat down on the bed, all prepared to tell Ma about the exciting revelation of the new, athletic Mr Candy and how the hooligans had been routed but Ma merely said:

'Don't bump about, Pop. Please.'

Pop was now quite certain that Ma must be feeling a bit dodgy and said:

'Sorry, Ma. What I came up to tell you about was something terrific that just happened in the marquee. Perfickly terrific. Mr Candy—'

'Not now. Later.'

Pop felt greatly mystified, even rebuffed. What made

it worse was that the idea of killing two birds with one stone clearly wasn't on any more. It was all a bit worrying and suddenly he leaned over Ma, kissed her very lightly on the forehead and said:

'Sure I can't get you a drop of somethink, Ma?'

'No, thanks. Just leave me.'

This, Pop thought, was a bit serious. Ma was obviously more than off colour. She wasn't often like this, he said, was she?

'Well, I have been once or twice.'

'Oh?' Pop said. 'How's that, then? Whatever's the matter, Ma?'

Ma turned in the bed. Her dark eyes were soft and sleepy.

'Oh! it's nothing very much,' she said, 'but somehow I don't think it'll be very long before we have another christening.'